TIE DIED

(A Bert Shambles Mystery)

by

Tim Hall

For information, email **Cozy Cat Press**, cozycatpress@aol.com or visit our website at: www.cozycatpress.com

COZY CAT
PRESS

ISBN: 978-1-939816-60-3

Printed in the United States of America

Cover design by Paula Ellenberger
http://www.paulaellenberger.com/

1 2 3 4 5 6 7 8 9 10

Acknowledgments

My sincere gratitude to the Mystery Writers of America, especially the New York Chapter and my friends there who have made the past couple of years so much fun. Thanks to Richie Narvaez, S.A. Solomon, Jeff Markowitz, Dru Ann, Charles Salzberg, Alex Segura, Angel Colon, Thomas Pluck, Scott Adlerberg, Gerald Butler, Joseph Goodrich, Cathi Stoler, Todd Robinson, and the rest of the Noir At The Bar and Thuglit crowds. Special thanks to my advance readers for their time and thoughtful attention: Todd, Diane, Tohoru, Elizabeth, David, Jen, and Jessica. As always, this book would not have been possible without the love and support of Mary and George. Thank you.

Dedicated to my mom, Carolyn K. Hall—a rock and roller in her own way, from way back.

CHAPTER 1: MID AUGUST-ISH

I used to think that being poor was the worst thing that could happen to a guy. Then I got a taste of the spotlight and I saw that fame was even worse. But it wasn't until I was staring into the smoking eye sockets of the electrocuted hippie that I finally understood: the worst thing of all is being dead.

A small crowd of concertgoers had gathered at the foot of the stage. Some were crying, some looked too stoned to care. The rest were tweeting pictures of the dead guy.

There was another pop, followed by a sizzling sound and the smell of burning skin. Someone pointed.

"His beard's on fire."

I stepped on the small flame, leaving a muddy footprint on his right cheek. *Sorry, dude.*

At that time I still didn't know what the dead hippie had to do with the sweaty memorabilia dealer, rare guitars, or a biker gang from Maine, but, of course, they were all connected. I just didn't know it yet.

My companion turned to me, her face blank with shock.

"I'll understand if you don't want to help me with the garage sale," she said.

Maybe I should back up a bit.

Twenty-four hours earlier I had been standing in line at the Mumfrey library, waiting to check out some movies, when I felt a tap on my shoulder. I ignored it, thinking it was probably just another weirdo.

Ever since I was featured on the news for helping to solve a crime, this kind of thing has been happening to me. I've learned that even a tiny bit of celebrity brings the crazies out of the woodwork. I came home once and found a bug-eyed guy camped on the lawn, babbling about UFOs. I got love letters from the sort of women who write marriage proposals to death row amputees. One lady said she was going to leave her home in Georgia for the first time in seven years and come up to Long Island to visit me, just as soon as she could find someone to remove the door of her trailer so she could fit through. That's why, when I felt the tapping, I closed my eyes and hoped the person behind me would go away. She didn't.

"Hey!"

I turned, ready to tell the person to buzz off. To my surprise, I saw a lovely face smiling back at me, bright blue eyes framed by a full and shining head of wavy blonde hair. She was wearing tight cut-off jeans and a tie-dyed T-shirt with colorful splotches everywhere and a ring of dancing bears in the center. She even had all her teeth.

"Are you Bert Shambles?"

I nodded.

"I knew it! I recognized you from the news!" She turned to the woman standing next to her, a serious-looking brunette who was dressed in a more athletic style, like she'd just come from the gym. "I told you it was him." Her friend looked disinterested.

"That was a really brave thing you did, it's such an incredible story."

"Thank you."

She looked at my injured arm and touched the cast, gently. "You were hurt. I remember now."

"Nothing major. The cast is coming off soon."

The line moved up. The woman craned her head around and looked at the DVDs in my good hand.

"*Highlander, Willow, Conan, the Barbarian.* Learning some new moves to fight off the bad guys?" She karate-chopped the air, then laughed at her own joke. I couldn't help but smile.

I nodded at the books in her arms. "Your turn."

She held them up, one at a time. They had titles like *eBay For Dummies*, *How to Start a Business on Etsy*, and *Garage-Sale-o-nomics 101*.

"Learning how to knit?" I said.

"Bingo," she laughed.

It was my turn to check out. The blonde came alongside me.

"Be nice to this guy," she said to the clerk. "He's a local hero."

The clerk gave me the stink eye, then checked out the DVDs, then the blonde pushed her books over. She stuck out her hand and we shook.

"I'm Scarlet, by the way."

"Hello, Scarlet *Bytheway*. Nice meeting you."

"Totally. You look a lot younger in person. How old are you, like 20?"

"23."

"I'm 37. That's old, right?"

"Not at all," I lied.

"You're just being nice."

I wasn't just being nice, not entirely. Scarlet was gorgeous, and looked a lot younger than 37. She had the kind of genes that would make her beautiful no matter how old she was. I bet she'd still be turning heads at 40.

"I like your bears."

"My what?" She looked down. "Oh, thanks. I admit it, I'm a hippie. The Dead are my favorite band."

"Is that the…Grateful Dead?"

"Oh, man, now you're making me feel old. Yes, the one and the same. Our parents were big Deadheads. We were both named for their favorite songs. My parents called me Scarlet, after "Scarlet Begonias," and China's parents named her for "China Cat Sunflower.""

"Don't remind me," China muttered.

"It could be worse," Scarlet laughed. "Their favorite song could have been "Friend of the Devil.""

"I'd like Devil better," her friend answered.

"I was thinking Friend," Scarlet answered. "And hey, my brother got it even worse. They called him Dew."

Scarlet finished with the clerk, then China checked out a book. China seemed uncomfortable. I tried breaking the ice.

"What are you reading?"

She shrugged and showed me the book. "Stuff about video editing."

"Chi is working on an amazing project."

"Scar, don't."

"Why not? Bert's a famous guy, maybe he can get you some media contacts to promote the series. Okay, I won't embarrass you." Scarlet turned to me. "Trust me, it's really cool."

"I have to get back to the studio," China said. "I'll catch you later, Scar. Nice meeting you, Bert."

"Likewise."

"Hold up, Chi. I'll come with you."

Scarlet reached into her bag and pulled out a piece of paper and a pen. She wrote down a phone number, then handed me the paper.

"There's a music festival tomorrow. My friend's band is playing. Give me a call if you want to go. I'm heading out there around four o'clock."

She shook my hand firmly.

"See you around, Bert Shambles."

I watched her go. Scarlet bounced off alongside China. She held her books against her chest like a schoolgirl. For once I felt warm and good inside after meeting a stranger. There was a rhythm to the way she walked, like she was dancing to music that only she could hear. And I don't mean in the same way as the crazies who sometimes camped on my lawn and yelled at the clouds. Scarlet didn't strike me as crazy, she just seemed very happy. But I had been wrong before.

I looked at the paper she'd given me. Even her handwriting looked happy; the characters were loopy and loose and nice to look at. I turned it over and read the other side. There was a very badly drawn naked man and woman holding hands, who I assumed were meant to represent Adam and Eve. None of the good parts were showing; they were covered by the leaves and branches of a tree with a snake coming out of it, an apple in its mouth. Under that, in a wavy, hard-to-read font it said:

Phunky Phreak Phestival
Pheaturing
PHOWL
Shawnasee State Park
Admission Phree

It gave the date and time. A website for directions and questions.

My first thought was that I'd rather have a root canal than stand around some park with a bunch of stoners, listening to corny music while getting sunstroke. Just thinking about it put me in a bad mood. But by the time I got home I felt differently. It wasn't like I was getting lots of invitations to go places; in fact, it was the first invitation I'd gotten anywhere in a long time, if you don't count the marriage proposals from morbidly obese trailer-park invalids. My girlfriend was three thousand miles away and there was no telling when—or if—she'd be coming back. I remembered something my therapist, Dr. Kornbluth, had said to me during one of our sessions: *Don't be the kind of person who treats his loneliness with isolation.* I could relate to that.

I got back to my room and put the DVDs on the small desk that holds the battleship gray Royal manual typewriter that I use to write my journal. Then I sat on the cot and looked at the flyer again. I thought of Scarlet's bright smile, her laughing manner. Being around her had relaxed me. Now that I was home, alone, I could feel the walls of the room closing in around me.

I looked up at the framed picture Aria had sent me, of her on the beach in San Diego in a white bikini. I felt guilty. The picture was on the dresser next to the TV and Blu-ray player she'd sent me, to keep me entertained during my recovery. She was the most gorgeous woman I had ever laid eyes on, and the most generous. I was crazy about her, and she said she was still crazy about me, but a long-distance relationship was hard on both of us—especially since we'd only had a few days together before she had to go to California because of family problems. To be honest, I kind of liked sitting around moping about it, but it clearly wasn't doing me any good. If a woman who thought I was a hometown hero wanted to invite me to a concert, what was the problem? I was sure Aria would understand. Especially if she never found out about it.

CHAPTER 2: THE NOT THIN MAN

The next day I got to Scarlet's at four. She'd been just as sweet on the phone as she'd been at the library, and was excited when I told her I'd like to join her. The front door opened as I was halfway up the walk. Scarlet greeted me with a big smile.

"Come into my lair, little boy."

There was a cozy entry way, with a staircase going up on one side, and two arched openings leading into other rooms. Scarlet led me through one of the arches, into the family room. There was something about the place that reminded me of the Hobbit house in the *Lord of the Rings* movies. It was wooden and homey, quiet and dark without being depressing. The shelves around the room were filled with old record albums. There had to be thousands of them. There were little tables and lamps scattered around, and beautiful, thick rugs covering the floor completely, in deep red and golden patterns.

In the center, a well-worn brown leather sectional surrounded a large wood and glass coffee table, on top of which sat a silver Apple laptop. The pile of library books was next to the laptop. I felt totally at peace the moment I entered. It was the kind of room I wanted to sink into and never leave.

"Do you want something to drink? A beer?"

"Water's fine."

"Make yourself at home. I'll be right back."

I walked around the room, looking at the shelves of records. I've always been fascinated by how other people live, probably because my own home life had been pretty sketchy at times. My dad left when I was not quite three, never to be seen or heard from again, and my mom had struggled to raise me the best she could. She had a good long-term job with a local attorney, working in his office, so we never starved but we never had much beyond that, either.

Scarlet came back into the living room with two glasses of ice water. She handed me one.

"I wanted to ask you something. What's your job situation like?"

"I work part-time at the St. Boniface thrift shop, but I don't go back until after Labor Day."

"I thought I remembered something like that. How would you like to earn some extra cash in the meantime? It's not very exciting. It would probably seem dull to a hometown hero like you."

"Try me."

She motioned around the room.

"This place. Everything. I need to sell as much as I can, so I can finally put the house on the market."

"You're selling this place?"

I had only been there a few minutes but I already felt a pain in my heart at the thought of that room going away.

"It's a bummer, but it's got to be done. My dad passed away earlier this year, and I have the swell job of disposing of everything and then splitting the proceeds with my brother in Florida. He's been really cool about it so far, but it can't drag on forever."

"What would I have to do?"

"You could help me organize and price the stuff. Some of it I'll probably list on eBay, or Etsy, or any other site that makes sense. And I'd like to have a big estate sale sometime in the next couple of months, before the weather turns cold. With your thrift shop experience you'd be perfect. Plus you seem really cool."

"It looks like a big job."

"Exactly. The whole house is filled, upstairs and down. The garage is filled too. Lots of boxes that haven't been opened or looked at in years, maybe decades. I don't think my brother really understands how overwhelming a job it is for one person, but I talked to him about it recently and he told me to hire whatever help I needed and then take half of the cost out of his share. What do you say?"

"I could use the extra money, but I don't know anything about selling stuff online. And I've never organized an estate sale before."

"Me neither! That's why I got those books out of the library. It's not rocket science. I'm sure the two of us could manage to figure it out. It'll be fun. I can't pay much, only fifteen an hour, but on the bright side I'm a pretty mellow boss."

We were interrupted by the doorbell. Scarlet went to answer it. Fifteen bucks an hour was a lot of money; it was more than I made at the thrift shop. I looked at the shelves, the records and old stereo equipment. I always loved going through people's stuff; it was the best part of my job at the thrift shop. It made me think about the people who had owned it, what they valued, and what I held onto and valued by comparison. I probably would have made a good garbage man.

"Hey! You can't just barge in here!"

Scarlet's cry was followed by the sound of the front door banging open.

"You've got to let me in!"

It was a man's voice. I ran out to the entryway and almost collided with the short, heavyset guy who was charging in. We both skidded to a stop and stumbled back a few steps. His face was sweaty, his eyes wide and crazy. I wondered for a second if he'd come to inform me of an alien invasion, but he looked at me in shock instead.

"Who are you?"

"None of your business." Scarlet spoke sharply. "I want you to leave. Now."

"But this is important!"

"Didn't you hear the lady? Get out. *Now*."

The sweaty guy turned again and looked back at me. Then he pivoted and ran out. He knocked into the door on the way out. The force of the impact caused a picture to fall off the wall; it crashed to the floor.

Scarlet went over and picked up the pieces of the broken frame. "I guess that's one less thing we have to worry about selling. What a jerk."

"What was that about?"

"His name's Martin Douglas. He's a memorabilia dealer. He runs Rosemary & Time."

"That sounds familiar."

"It's the nostalgia shop down by the dock. They carry old games, toys, that kind of stuff."

"I know that place."

"They also carry old records and rock and roll memorabilia, so I stopped by there a while back, to see if he'd be interested in making an offer on any of my dad's stuff. I brought a few samples and explained what I had."

"I bet he was glad to get a crack at this stuff."

"That's the strange thing. He wasn't interested at first. He made some ridiculously low offer for the vinyl, like ten cents a record, and only for the ones he decided to keep. I'm sure my dad had a lot of junk, but I know for a fact that some of these albums are worth more on their own than what he would have paid for the whole collection. Same with my dad's personal memorabilia, from his rock and roll days. He said that there was no market for my dad's personal musical items unless they had some clear connection to someone famous, like a concert poster that included Jimi Hendrix or Janis Joplin or someone like that."

"If he wasn't interested, what was he doing here?"

"That's where it gets even stranger. After blowing me off and telling me no, a few weeks ago he contacted me out of the blue. Wanted to meet right away. He was very interested all of a sudden. At first, I thought it was a sign, like my dad was somehow telling me that I had to move on and get his stuff out of here, so I had him come over to talk about it. Right away I got a really creepy vibe from the guy."

"How so? Apart from the fact that he's creepy, I mean."

"Right? For one thing, it was obvious he thought I was an idiot. He kept trying to put me in my place, said he needed to walk around the house by himself and appraise things before he gave me an answer. He was trying to shake me loose so he could have the run of the place. I told him that I wasn't comfortable letting a stranger go through my house unaccompanied and he was offended by that, so I figured I'd just let him poke around a bit. Pretty soon it became apparent that he was looking for something. I told him to stay out of my bedroom and then I heard a floorboard creak that only happens in my room, and I went upstairs. He was in my closet, rummaging around in my clothes!"

"He's definitely not your size. Is he a perv?"

"I don't know! I asked him what he was doing and he got really snotty with me, so I asked him again if there was anything specific he was looking for and he got even more snotty, so I kicked him out and told him I didn't want to do business with him. Right away he apologized and said he was under a lot of pressure, he was sorry and would never do that again, blah blah, but he still wasn't being honest. I knew he was holding something back from me. Since then he's been very persistent, he tries to make some kind of contact every few days. But he'd never done anything so bold before. I'm lucky you were here to scare him off."

"You mentioned your dad's personal music memorabilia. Was he in the music business?"

"Yup. He was in a band, back in the 1960s in San Francisco. He knew all those guys—the Dead, Janis, Jimi, the Airplane. Can you imagine? What an amazing time that must have been."

"Was he famous?"

"No, he never made it as a rock star. He had a band called the Peppermint Wristwatch. They were on the verge of making it big, had a major record label interested and everything. Then the singer died unexpectedly, from smoking pot."

"I didn't know you could overdose on pot."

"You can't. He drowned in his bong water."

"How is that possible?"

"It was a really big bong."

Scarlet shook her head and chuckled.

"It sure was a different world back then."

"What did your dad do after that?"

"He started a new band, which didn't last long, then he tried to get other things going, but nothing stuck. He was pretty shaken up by the singer dying and the band losing a record deal when they were so close. By the time he got himself back together the moment had passed, I think. These colorful historical periods can have a big impact but they're usually much smaller and more fragile than people realize. My dad said that the so-called Summer of Love, which kicked off the whole flower-power movement, actually happened after the real scene was already over. After that it was just tourists and theater, a theme park. The real creativity had moved on. So he did, too."

"Where's your mom?"

"She died when I was six. Car accident. Drunk driver hit her."

"That's sad. I'm sorry to hear that."

"What can you do? She was a sweet lady, a real flower child. They went to Woodstock, followed the Dead for years, all that tree-hugger stuff."

"Did your dad remarry?"

She shook her head. "Nope. There were girlfriends here and there, some really wonderful ones too. They'd stick around for a while then move on, for whatever reason. Probably because they knew he wouldn't commit to them. For all the talk about free love, most of the flower children were looking for the same things that mainstream people want: marriage, family, a nice place to live. He just couldn't put himself or us through that again. He felt like he lost the two great loves of his life, first the band and then my mom."

"So how did you guys get by? This is a pretty nice house."

"My dad was adaptable. That was one of his best qualities, I think. He reinvented himself. He used his musical talent and good looks and charm to get a gig at an advertising company in the city. He did really well at that, because he was a clever writer from all his years of songwriting. He wrote a few jingles that did extremely well and made him a lot in royalties. He wound up with a big job at a top firm. For as long as I could remember he was just a guy who took the train into the city every day, then came home at night."

"It must have been rough, trying to raise two kids on his own."

"I'm sure it was, but we never knew it. He was always happy. My brother and I are like that too. We had a series of nannies who helped raise us. Mostly young women he knew through his music connections, or his West Coast days. There was always some beautiful, barefoot young woman bopping around the house, with a name like Sunshine or Daffodil, making buckwheat pancakes or bean sprout sandwiches." She chuckled. "I think I subconsciously wanted to emulate those women, which is why I became a full-blown hippie chick. They were always so awesome to me and my brother and I just worshiped them."

"No wonder he didn't get remarried. With all those babes around he didn't have to."

"Ha! That's good. I've often wondered about that. It was his choice to make, and I don't think me or my brother ever felt deprived. I had a really wonderful childhood, despite the difficult circumstances. Then again, I never got married, so maybe there was something about his need for freedom, or avoiding pain that I took from the experience."

"It could have been a lot worse."

"Exactly. Look at someone like China. What a hard time that poor girl has had. And both her parents are alive."

"What do you mean?"

"Her mom left when she was young, and remarried some guy who was horrible to China. Then she tried living with her dad, but he was messed up on drugs and alcohol. He wound up in prison for a long time."

"How do you know her?"

"Her dad, Charlie, was in the Peppermint Wristwatch with my dad, Dave. Charlie was the bass player, and my dad played guitar and sang. They had grown up together in Michigan, before heading West to make it big. My mom and China's mom, meanwhile, were originally from New York. They were also good friends and major Deadheads. Charlie and Janine,

China's mom, started dating first, and she introduced Dave to my mom, Bernadette. I think China's parents settled out here first, then my mom and dad followed a couple of years later."

"And your family thrived while theirs kind of went downhill."

"Exactly. I know my dad was always loyal to Charlie; he really loved him like a brother. But Charlie couldn't adjust to life after the band the way my dad did. I know my mom's death was a huge part of it. Before he died my dad told me that her death was the worst thing that ever happened to him, as well as the best. It forced him to grow up and really accept life on life's terms, be grateful for what he had and not sweat the stuff he didn't have. But Charlie couldn't deal with being an adult. He was always starting things and walking away from them. Then he got mixed up in drugs, and you know how that goes."

"Where's Charlie now?"

"He was in prison for a long time, like almost ten years. I'm not sure where he is now. China doesn't like to talk about it; it makes her really upset. Her mom moved to Maryland years ago, with her second husband."

Scarlet looked at her phone.

"We better get going. I don't want to miss Phowl."

I waited by the door as Scarlet got her bag and keys and locked up. When we got outside she saw the Olds parked in front.

"That yours?"

"Yup."

"Wow, sweet ride. Do you want to drive or should I?"

"I can drive."

"On second thought, let's take my car. Save the earth and all that. People see me driving up in that gas-

guzzler and all the environmental hippies will freak."
She flashed me a devilish grin.
"That might be kind of fun, actually."

CHAPTER 3: PHUNKY PHREAKS

We took her car. It was a twenty minute drive to
Shawnasee State Park. We were quiet most of the way.
I was still mulling over what that big jerk, Martin, had
done. I had to watch my temper. I see a woman being
bullied or threatened and I tend to freak out and start
swinging. That's what got me into trouble, and wound
up with me being stuck back in Mumfrey.

"Have you ever heard Phowl before?"

"No, but the name sounds familiar."

"A lot of people get them confused with Phish, who
are much bigger and better known. Don't tell my friend
Gavin I said that if you meet him. He's really sensitive
about it. He claims Trey Anastasio stole the whole Ph-
thing from him."

"I won't say a word."

"Do you mind if I put on one of their CDs?"

"Feel free."

"I'm not into their newer stuff so much, but I really
loved their first few albums. I knew those guys at the
University of Maine when they were first starting out.
We all went to school together. Those were such fun
days. My dad co-produced their first album, in fact,
though he refused to take any money or credit it for it,
of course. To thank him they recorded a couple of his
Peppermint Wristwatch songs, which was a huge thrill
for him."

Scarlet put on the CD. The music buzzed and
swirled and crashed. I wanted to like it because she
liked it and I liked her, but I wasn't sure what to think. I
usually have to listen to things a few times before I can

make up my mind. It felt good just to be going somewhere new, doing something different. I was always getting into ruts, but Scarlet struck me as the type of person who never would.

"Hey, I haven't even asked you. What kind of music do you like?"

"I don't know. Anything, I guess."

"Come on, what kind of answer is that? A young guy like you, you've got to be into something, you don't live in a cave."

"I kind of like Katy Perry."

"Really? I wouldn't have guessed. She's pretty adorable, though."

My phone buzzed in my pocket. It was Aria. I sent the call to voicemail.

"Who was that? Girlfriend?"

There was a playful tone in Scarlet's voice. It made my cheeks burn.

"Aw, don't be embarrassed. I remember something about that on the news. Didn't you save her life or something?"

"That might be a slight exaggeration, but yes, that's her."

"I'm sorry, I should have told you to bring her along as well."

"She's in California for the summer, maybe longer."

"Bummer for you, lucky for me." She gave me a playful nudge with her elbow. "Here we are."

We got to the entrance of the park. There was a line of cars ahead of us, but it moved fairly quickly. Scarlet paid the parking fee, then followed the signs until we came to a field, with different lots separated by metal stakes and white rope. Guys holding bright orange sticks and wearing matching reflective vests directed us into an open row. We locked the car, then crossed the hot open field with the other recent arrivals, in the direction of the stage. People carried folding chairs and coolers. Some people wore big sun hats or colorful outfits; there was a lot of tie-dye.

We had arrived between acts. Music was being pumped through the P.A. system, some kind of heavy rock that I didn't recognize. It was a pretty mellow scene. I don't know what I was expecting. Not Woodstock, but I imagined tents, jugglers, dudes wearing face paint with topless women on their shoulders. It wasn't like that. There were a couple hundred or so mostly normal-looking people there, milling around. Once in a while I caught the whiff of something that definitely wasn't tobacco. Some shirtless guys flipped Frisbees around. There was only one juggler.

"Let's go find Gavin," Scarlet said. "They're probably getting ready to go on soon."

There was a fence in front of the stage, creating about a ten-foot gap between it and the crowd. We followed the fencing along the far side of the stage, where there was a narrow gap. There was a bored-looking security guy sitting there, wearing a black polo shirt with a little insignia on it and holding a walkie-talkie. Scarlet floated over to him and worked her charms. The guy listened, talked into the walkie-talkie, listened for a reply, then smiled and waved her in. She motioned to me and I followed her.

The stage was set up on what looked like scaffolding. Four taller posts rose from the corners of the stage. They were connected by crossbeams holding lights that were tilted at different angles.

We passed a row of Porta-Potties. Scarlet motioned with her thumb.

"I'd better use the girls' room. Do you mind?"

"Have fun."

Scarlet bopped off in her dancing way. She went into one of the plastic units and the green disc turned to red.

I took in the scene while I waited. Behind the toilets a hundred yards or so there was a large 18-wheel truck. It was being used as a generator, judging by the thick black cables that were coming out of the side of it and the large signs warning HIGH VOLTAGE—DANGER plastered on the side. There were various technicians walking around, barking orders or listening to someone else bark orders at them. I saw a guy tuning a guitar, and several large plastic bins filled with ice and bottles of water.

I saw a tall, thin guy who I assumed was one of the musicians, judging by his groovy clothing, long hair and beard. He was having an animated conversation with someone else, who I couldn't quite see until the tall guy shifted. I had to look twice to be sure.

It was Martin, the sweaty memorabilia dealer who'd pushed his way into Scarlet's house.

I was too far away to hear what they were saying, but it was clearly an intense conversation. The musician guy was leaning down slightly, using his hands and arms for emphasis. It looked like he was trying to argue without losing his cool. The sweaty memorabilia guy was arguing back, jabbing a finger into his other palm to emphasize his points.

Scarlet came bouncing up.

"Thanks for waiting. Let's find Gavin before they go on."

"Well, well, if it's not Miss Scarlet."

Scarlet mumbled a curse, then turned around. There were six of them, in sizes ranging from big to huge to ridickyballs. They wore leather or denim jackets with the sleeves cut off. Most of them were wearing jeans, but a couple of guys wore leather pants, which I imagined must be hard to take in the summer heat. One guy was wearing leather chaps over his jeans. The biggest guy in front was wearing leather head to toe, with a cut-off denim vest over his leather jacket. He had dirty blond hair almost to his shoulders and a few days' worth of beard. Scarlet glared at him.

"What do you want, Lizard?"

I thought she was insulting him, then I saw a patch that was sewn over the front pocket of the denim that said "Lizard."

"You know what I want, pretty lady. Just what's owed to me. I think you and I better talk after the show."

Scarlet folded her arms tight and looked away. The goons sauntered by. When they passed, I saw the backs of their jackets. There was a big patch that took up the center panel. It was an image of a wheel, except instead of rubber there was a snake in a perfect circle, eating its own tail. There were lightning bolts shooting out from the snake. Over that, in gothic writing it said *Electric Wheels*, and underneath it said *Dirigo*.

"Jerks."

"What was that about?"

"Nothing. They're just troublemakers. They follow the band around on a lot of its tours, acting as stagehands and whatever else."

"What does 'Dirigo' mean?"

"It's Latin for 'I lead' or 'I direct.' It's the state motto of Maine."

"That Lizard guy seemed to know you. What did he want?"

"It's nothing. Ancient history. Some guys just never grow up. Come on. Let's find Gavin."

We found him on the other side of the stage, in a hospitality tent that had been set up for the bands. It was the same guy I saw arguing with Martin earlier. He looked lost in thought until he saw Scarlet, then his face lit up and he ran over and hugged her so hard he lifted her off her feet. When he finally put her down, Scarlet waved herself with her hand as if to keep herself from fainting, then let out a big laugh.

"Gavin, I want you to meet Bert. Bert, this is Gavin. He's one of my oldest friends."

"What's up, dude? Glad to meet you." He had a firm handshake and a gleam in his eye. "Any friend of Scarlet's is a friend of mine. She's an awesome chick."

"We just wanted to wish you luck, Gav. Have a great show."

Gavin took her by the hand.

"I need to talk to you about something. You sticking around after?"

"Sure."

"Cool. Come backstage and find me. Don't forget. It's important."

One of the Electric Wheels bikers came over. "You're on in five," he told Gavin.

"Give my friends here a good spot on the side of the stage, okay?"

The biker shrugged, then motioned to us. "Come with me."

Scarlet was elated. She looped her arm in mine and did her hip-shake walk. "Didn't I tell you he was cool?"

We followed the biker up some metal steps, to the side of the stage behind some big P.A. speakers.

"You two can watch from here," he instructed. "Don't touch anything. And if anyone asks what you're doing here tell them Anaconda said it was okay."

We watched him go. "What's these guys obsession with reptiles?" I asked. Scarlet laughed.

"Beats me. Look, I think they're about to start."

Fog started filtering in from the sides of the stage, courtesy of some hidden machines. The crowd started cheering. It had gotten a lot bigger in the short time since we'd arrived and I could see more streaming in from the parking lot. There were a few hundred people now at least. The afternoon was getting close to that magic hour, and the park and everything in it looked green and fresh and beautiful.

We were in the perfect spot to watch the show. Scarlet squeezed my arm in excitement.

"I'd forgotten how much I love going to concerts. This brings back so many wonderful memories. Thank you for being here with me."

There was a definite change in the energy of the crowd; something good was about to happen. From the other side of the stage the MC came out and stood at the microphone. After a little flare of feedback, he bellowed into the mic.

"All right, we're now ready for the highlight of the Phunky Phreak Phestival!" The crowd cheered. "Our next band comes all the way down from Bangor, Maine…and they're here to blow your minds! So please put your hands together and give a big Long Island welcome for…PHOWL!"

The crowd roared. More fog drifted in, covering the floor of the stage. The band came out and waved to the crowd, took their instruments. The drummer counted off and they started a slow, spacey introduction. There was a swirly organ sound and the drummer hammered his cymbals with mallets. The bass player ran his fingers up the neck and tapped out a few ringing notes. Finally, Gavin came out, holding a guitar. Scarlet and the rest of the fans cheered louder. She turned to me, smiling.

"I'm so excited!" she screamed.

I was excited too. Gavin looked every inch like a rock star. It wasn't just his skinny frame and long hair, or the velvet pants, suede booties, and paisley tunic that came down past his waist. It was the confidence he carried it with, the feeling he projected that he was completely at home up on stage. Maybe that's all people really responded to, confidence and style. Maybe that was what separated the rock stars and celebrities from the rest of us. I'm sure having a bit of talent doesn't hurt either, which is something I don't have. I've been told I look like a young Jack White, which is a pretty big compliment, but with my drab work clothes and hangdog expression, most people would probably think I'm more roadie than rock star.

The music got louder and more intense. Gavin closed his eyes and swayed in time to the music, then swung his arm and started slashing noisy chords on the guitar. Then he walked up to the microphone to sing.

And that's when everything went bonkers.

There was a loud noise, almost like a bang, and a puff of smoke. I thought it was part of the show until I saw the expression on the singer's face. His body tensed and twisted, and I could see smoke coming off of his body. Then he flew backwards and collapsed in front of the drum riser. There was another loud bang, and the amps and P.A. system suddenly went dead.

The keyboard player was the first to run over. Then a couple of stagehands ran onto the stage and hunched over him. Scarlet cried out her friend's name and rushed over to his side.

That's when I heard the first scream, loud and terrifying. It took me a second to realize it was coming from me.

CHAPTER 4: A SHOCKING DEVELOPMENT

It was chaos onstage but also oddly calm—a strange combination of noise and silence, motion and stillness at the same time. I floated over to Scarlet and stood next to her. She was kneeling by Gavin, clearly afraid to touch him in case he was still electrified, crying and calling his name. I made a quick scan of the surrounding area and didn't see any wires connecting him to anything—even the plug in his guitar had been pulled out when he flew back—but the power to the stage had shut off completely.

As I pointed my foot over his cheek and put out the sizzling spot on his beard, an unsettling thought hit me. I knew there was no connection between me and Gavin, and that I had no part in what had just happened, but somewhere deep in my gut I got the feeling that before it was all over I was somehow going to be involved.

"Clear the stage! Clear the stage!"

The bikers barked orders; someone ran over with a first aid kit, and I saw one of the bikers shove the person away angrily. I couldn't blame either of them—the person who was just trying to help, or the biker for not tolerating it. It wasn't like Gavin had the kind of injuries that you could put some ointment and a Band-Aid on. Considering how much juice went through the scrawny singer, I doubted if Dr. Frankenstein could help him now.

I saw the ambulance bouncing across the field, coming toward the stage with lights going. I took Scarlet by the arm. She looked up at me, lost, and said it would be okay if I didn't want to help her with her garage sale. I knew she was in shock. People sometimes say or do strange things at those times.

"We can talk about it later. We'd better go."

Two of the bikers started herding people off the stage. As we got to the bottom of the stairs, two EMS workers hustled by us quickly, carrying a gurney and some kind of medical bag. We stood off to the side of the grassy area just behind the stage until we saw the EMS workers carrying him off on the gurney. They loaded him onto the ambulance and drove off, lights and sirens blaring. I didn't know if it was the uneven terrain of the field or Gavin's condition, but they didn't seem to be in a hurry.

As soon as the ambulance left, the reality of what we'd just witnessed finally hit me. The short circuit had blown out the sound system, but it wasn't until the ambulance's siren trailed off in the distance that the terrible silence hanging over the stage became overwhelming. In some ways it seemed scarier than what had just happened.

Tears streamed down Scarlet's face. She looked lost and bewildered.

"I can't believe this. What happened? Does anybody know if they can save him?"

One of the bikers walked by, wheeling a large road case. I stopped and asked him what Gavin's condition was. He shrugged.

"I don't know, man. Last I heard, he wasn't breathing. No pulse."

"Did the EMS guys revive him?"

"Maybe in the ambulance. I don't know."

I thanked him and he walked away.

"If he wasn't breathing for that long, would it even matter?" Scarlet was talking to me. "Would he be a vegetable?"

"I don't know. Let's wait until we have more accurate information. Maybe the band will know."

"The band. That's right. I can't go without talking to those guys. Do you mind?"

"Of course not."

We made our way through the confusion behind the stage. There were already a couple of cops on the scene, uniformed officers taking a statement from Lizard. He looked angry, and was motioning a lot with his hands. I didn't like the guy. I didn't see the memorabilia dealer anywhere.

We found the rest of the band in a bus parked behind the equipment truck. It was a small bus, like the kind they use for shuttles at the airport. Two of the band members were outside, talking sullenly. I recognized them as the drummer and bass player. Scarlet went over and hugged them both, then introduced us.

"This is Tommy and Ben. This is my friend Bert."

We nodded politely. Nobody felt much like social pleasantries.

"Is Brent around?"

"In the bus," Tommy said. We went up inside. We found Brent, the keyboard player, lying on a ratty couch that had been installed along the wall of the van. Above that were sleeping bunks. Clothes were thrown or piled everywhere. When he saw her coming, Brent started to get up but she went down to him and hugged him tight.

"I can't believe it," she whispered. "It's unbelievable."

"I can believe it." Brent's voice was clearer and stronger than I expected. He pulled away from Scarlet and looked at her. "I knew something bad was going to happen one of these days."

"What do you mean?"

He picked up a pack of cigarettes from the floor, took one out of the pack and lit it with a lighter he was holding in his other hand.

"Look at the people around us."

"What do you mean?" Scarlet asked. Brent grunted, took a drag from his cigarette, exhaled and stared off into space.

"Nothing. Forget I said it." Scarlet accepted this at face value but there was something in the way that he said it that made me feel it was too important to let go.

"Are you talking about that biker gang, the Wheels or whatever they're called?"

He took another drag then stared at me.

"You really think what happened out there was an accident?"

"That's enough out of you." The voice that spoke was so gruff and forceful that we all jumped. I looked over and saw Lizard, the head biker, standing in the open door at the front of the van. He looked scary enough outside, but seeing him inside an enclosed space with no other easy exit was downright terrifying. He jabbed a finger at Brent.

"Don't be spouting any stupid conspiracy theories when the cops come and question you, or you might say something you later regret." Then he glared at me and Scarlet. "You two. Get the hell out and don't let me catch you back here again."

We didn't need to be told twice. We walked in stunned silence back to Scarlet's car. She finally fished the keys out of her bag with some difficulty. Her hands were shaking so badly that she couldn't unlock the door.

"Let me."

I took the keys and unlocked the driver side. Scarlet threw her arms around me and started sobbing.

"I'll drive us back," I said. "But I need you to tell me the best way."

Scarlet sniffled and thanked me and went around to the passenger side. I let her in, found the seat adjustment lever and pushed it back, adjusted the mirrors, then backed out and started for home. It looked like we were just in time; the stoners and hippies had finally realized that there was not going to be any more music for the day, and the crowds were beginning to fill up the parking lot. None of them looked in a hurry to go. There were a number of people crying, women mostly but more than a few men. Some people had started a drum circle, and there was such an energy and passion to the playing, or maybe desperation, that I sensed it was a different form of crying.

Scarlet shuddered.

"That smell. I'm never going to get it out of my nostrils."

"Just focus on getting us back."

"Keep straight. You're fine. I'll tell you when the next turn is."

"Were you and Gavin very close?"

"Not so much in recent years, but at one time we were. We met in college and we stayed pretty close while I was living in Maine, until near the end of my time there. They were always on the road, building a fan base. They almost seemed ready to break into the big time about ten years ago, but that fizzled out. The life of a musician is so hard; it takes so much effort and coordination for so little payoff."

"What happened near the end of your time in Maine? Did you two have a falling-out?"

"Sort of. It's kind of hard to explain. I love it up there, and really thought I could settle there permanently, but a lot of my friends never moved on after college. They didn't marry or start families, get careers or start businesses. That's fine, because I didn't really want those things either; what I guess I mean is that they didn't have any ambition, or dreams they were willing to work toward. They just wanted to smoke pot and act like their youth would last forever, in a perpetual party mode. And then other drugs started entering the picture. Harder stuff. Then it wasn't so innocent any more. That's when the bikers started hanging around, and a whole seedy underbelly kind of formed in the band's shadow. I tried to warn Gavin about it but he was too idealistic, so I kind of kept my distance."

"What do you think he wanted to see you about?"

"What do you mean?"

"He asked you to stick around after the show, to talk about something. He said it was important."

Scarlet cocked her head to one side. The streaks left by the dried tears were still evident.

"Did he? That's right, he did. I have no idea what he wanted. I hadn't spoken to him since shortly after my dad died. He was really sweet about it. That was like six, seven months ago. We hadn't spoken again until this afternoon. And now he's gone. I'll probably never know what he wanted to talk about."

"When you were in the bathroom I saw him talking to that memorabilia dealer who came by your house."

"Martin? That guy is a doofus. He was probably trying to get some inside access to band stuff that he could sell. Phowl aren't a big name but they're probably big enough that he could make a few bucks. Especially if they ever had a hit song or made the news."

"Like now?"

"Exactly. Take the next right."

"I can get us back from here. Thanks."

I didn't say any more about it. Maybe Gavin was in trouble and knew he could trust Scarlet. Maybe it was something Martin said to him backstage. Maybe his cat just had kittens and he wanted her to adopt one of them. It could have been anything.

I pulled into the driveway of Scarlet's house and turned off the engine. We got out of the car and Scarlet came around and hugged me.

"I'm sorry I dragged you into this. I thought it was going to be a fun day."

"Do you want me to stay for a while?"

"No, that's all right. I'll be fine. It's probably better if I'm alone now. But would you come back tomorrow? Maybe we could start organizing my dad's stuff. How's five o'clock?"

"Are you sure you're up for that?"

"Yes. I feel a strange sense of purpose about it now, like it's important that I don't put it off any longer. Life is too short, and we never know when it might suddenly be taken from us."

"See you tomorrow then, five o'clock."

She leaned over and kissed me on the cheek. I watched as she went up the walk and into the house, then I got into the Olds and headed for home.

CHAPTER 5: SAY WHAT

At the end of a dead-end street not far from the Mumfrey train station, last house on the right, is the rooming-house where I live. I rent a small room for $75 a week, which sounds like a good deal until you get a look at the place. Every fixture, knob, faucet, and peeling piece of wallpaper still stubbornly clinging to the grimy walls looks original to the 1930s when the house was built.

The landlord could probably get more for the land than the measly rent he gets from me and Aku, the only two tenants in his death-trap of a flophouse, but he keeps the place going for reasons that are probably best known only to him. He comes by to collect the rent once a month, cash only. The slightest mention of something that needs fixing gives him major spazz attacks. He goes running back to his smoking Buick and gurgles away until the next month, muttering in some foreign language that makes him sound like a villain from one of those cheesy Cold War movies from the 1980s.

I pushed open the front door—the lock was still broken more than six weeks after my girlfriend's brothers broke it open one night while they were looking to beat me up—and went up the crooked, creaking stairs to the second floor. The hallway was barely illuminated by a bare bulb so dim and sputtering that it must have been imported from whatever former Soviet republic my landlord came from. I was fishing the keys out of my pocket when I heard a cough behind me, to my left. It was my neighbor, Aku.

Aku is the resident Wizard in the rooming-house. A strange dude, but totally cool. He makes his living as a telephone psychic, reading tarot cards and tea leaves for the crazy old bats who pay a few bucks a minute to talk to him. He really loves what he does, and completely believes it's legit—so much so that he always wears a purple wizard robe that's covered with shiny stars and moons. Aku just kind of appears and disappears at will, which is hard considering he's well over six feet tall and has all this hair and these long fingernails. I don't know how he does it. I've never seen him actually come or go from the rooming-house, so I don't know if he only wears his robe while he works, but if I ever run into him in the supermarket and he's dressed like that I'm totally pretending I don't know him.

"Hello, Bert. There was a man from the cable company here earlier. I let him into your room. I hope that was all right."

"Fine," I said, not hearing him. I was trying to unlock the door, but my hand was shaking too much to get the key into the lock. I stopped what I was doing, closed my eyes and took a deep breath, the way Dr. K taught me to do when I was feeling stressed.

"I saw a guy get electrocuted today."

"Did you say electrocuted? If you're making a joke then I'm afraid I don't understand."

"It's not a joke. I was out at the Phunky Phreak Phestival with this woman who's friends with the band Phowl."

"Oh, yes, I remember them. Sort of like Phish, if I recall."

"Right. We talked to the singer, Gavin, then he let us watch from the side of the stage, which was totally cool. Then he walked out and zap...electrocuted. Dead."

"Goodness! That's terrible. How did it happen?"

"I don't know. Some problem with the equipment, I guess. He stepped up to the microphone and flew back about ten feet. His beard was on fire. I stepped on it."

"That must have been terrible. Are you all right?"

"I'm still numb, but I'll be okay."

My hand finally found the keyhole. I turned the key and unlocked the door. Then it hit me.

"Why was the cable man here? I don't have cable."

I turned around but Aku had disappeared.

I went into my room and closed the door. There was an open box on the floor, from Long Island Cable. Instructions, receipts, and a remote control that looked like it could guide a spaceship.

I had given Aku a key to my place, in case I needed help while my left arm was in a cast. It was especially helpful once the boxes started arriving from Aria. Aku is home most days. He'd been helping with the boxes, bringing them upstairs and getting things opened and unpacked. I don't like feeling helpless, but it was great having someone I could trust so nearby.

The new cable box was on my dresser, wedged next to Aria's other gifts: the huge LED TV, fancy Blu-ray player, and framed picture of her in a white bikini, smiling from the beach at San Diego. The closet was filled with more stuff: his and her robes, embroidered with our initials; foofy scented candles I was afraid to burn because the house was in such bad shape that I worried the whole place might spontaneously explode; jars of fancy jams, spreads, and hot sauces—I used the hot sauce on the burritos I brought home from the 7-11 down the street. Stuff like that, and much more.

I knew I should be grateful for this latest gift, and all the rest, but I wasn't feeling it right then. Aria had no idea what I'd been through that day, but the resentment I was feeling had been building up in me over the past six weeks. I asked her to stop buying me stuff but she didn't listen. I felt like she was using material things to make up for the fact that she couldn't be with me, but it only made the feelings worse. This latest incident only seemed to drive home the point. While I'd been struggling with real issues like a broken arm, how to pay my rent, and now watching a person die in front of my eyes, Aria was flitting around San Diego in a white bikini, shopping like some crazy TV housewife. She was playing a role in her own reality show, while I was getting my butt kicked by actual reality every day.

What did I know about Aria, anyway? We had gone to high school together, though I didn't remember her until we met again at St. Boniface over the summer. Her dad was supposedly connected to the mob, maybe in a big way. Her brothers were hostile and rude to me—when they weren't actually chasing me around town trying to beat me up. I would face them all a thousand times just to see Aria again, but every new gift she sent only reinforced just how alone I was, and how lonely. I had hoped going to the Phestival would ease that loneliness a bit and it had—right until the point Gavin had gotten zapped.

I got out my phone to call Aria and saw that I had a message from her, from when I was in the car with Scarlet. In the message Aria spoke in a low, serious tone. *We need to talk. I have something to tell you, and I'm not sure how.*

It didn't sound good, whatever it was. My heart sank. Was she breaking up with me? Probably. A young, beautiful woman gets her first taste of freedom from her overbearing, controlling parents and gets to spend a summer in California with her cousins. What did I expect? I knew she was having the time of her life, and imagined her going out dancing every night, and playing beach volleyball during the day with guys named Dirk and Gonzo. There was no way the memory of a sad, poor local boy could compete with the excitement of being the new kid in a new town—especially if you were as gorgeous, stylish and rich as Aria.

As if on cue, the phone started buzzing in my hand. It was her. I took a deep breath and answered, slowly.

"Hello?"

"Were you ever going to call me?"

"What do you mean?"

"Did you get my message?"

"Yes, I just got home. I was trying to figure out this cable TV stuff."

"It came already? That's good. Don't get too excited, though. It was just a present for getting your cast off."

"My cast," I groaned. "I knew there was something I was forgetting."

"I thought your appointment was today."

"It was. I completely spaced."

"How could you? It's all you've been talking about for weeks, how excited you were to be getting it off."

"I don't know. I was out at the Phestival and I guess it slipped my mind."

"What festival?"

"The Phunky Phreak Phestival. It's out in Shawnasee State Park. It's a hippie rock thing."

"Hippie rock? That doesn't sound like your scene. Why did you do that instead of getting your cast off?"

"I don't know. Someone gave me a flyer and it sounded like fun."

"Some random person gave you a flyer? Who was it?"

"Nobody. Just this woman I met at the library."

"You went on a date with a woman you met at the library?"

"No! It wasn't a date. I was standing in line, and she recognized me, and then she gave me this flyer for the concert and I thought I'd check it out."

"So it was just a random meeting?"

"Yes. Then she hired me to do some organizing at her place. Her dad had like thousands of albums, they're all over the walls."

"I thought you talked to her at the library."

"I did. But I went over to her house before we went to the Phestival."

Now that the words had come out of my mouth I realized how the situation might, when seen in a certain light, look like it had been a date.

"I see. That's why you forgot to get your cast off? Is your new hippie girlfriend going to take it off with her *good vibes*?"

"Don't be ridiculous. She's much older. Practically elderly."

"How old?"

"Thirty-seven."

"That's not elderly. That's a woman in her prime. Is she attractive?"

"She's not horrible."

"I bet she isn't. Sounds like cougar material to me."

"Wait a second. How did this become an interrogation of me? You're the one who left the dramatic message, about how you needed to tell me something."

"I did, but now I don't think I should. I don't know if there's any point."

"Try me."

"Okay, but I have to make it quick. I'm on a boat and I'm going to lose signal soon, we're getting far...shore."

"What?"

"I said, I'm...boat and ...go soon....Losing sig..."

"Why are you on a boat?"

"We're...Catalina... weekend."

"Who's 'we'?"

"That's...I'm trying…"

"What? I lost you."

"I...right now...back to him."

My heart was pounding in my chest. "Who?"

"The guy...boat...is…"

She said something else but it was garbled.

"What did you say?"

This time she yelled it. There was no mistaking what she said. It was loud and clear.

"I'VE MET SOMEONE."

The line went dead.

CHAPTER 6: AFTERMATH OF A BREAKUP

The next morning I felt like I'd been run over by a half-ton pickup driven by a two-ton man.

The evening was fuzzy. I tried remembering what I'd done. Bits and pieces came back, slowly and painfully. After the call with Aria, I'd left my room in a kind of trance. I was on foot, because I never drive if I know I'm going to get drunk. I started at the place near the train station, where most of the clientele comes in the form of sad, middle-aged businessmen who stop off there for a snort or three before going home to the wife and kids. It was early on a Saturday night so the place was practically empty. I wondered if that would be me in a few years, coming home on the LIRR from the city, pulling into Mumfrey at 6:30, knowing that there was nothing for me at home but an estranged wife and three or four kids who barely grunted at me. Aria would be cold and distant and I wouldn't be able to say or do anything about it because of her powerful family and money and she'd know it and I'd know it and the truth would hang there between us like a tumor, growing bigger and more horrible every day. Or maybe I'd be the cold and distant one, maybe I'd realize that she was shallow and dull, or hated black people, or some other disgusting trait that I wouldn't be able to handle. I'd shrink away from her and the thought of touching her, and I'd turn to the bottle and she'd turn to pills and the pool boy. Ah, marriage.

Or maybe I had it all wrong, and she'd mature into the smart, loyal, tough and beautiful woman that she was turning out to be, and I would look back years from now and curse my stupidity for losing such an a amazing woman. That was even worse to think about.

I downed two vodkas with cranberry juice, smoked a couple of cigarettes, then moved on to the next bar. Either the drinks were strong or my emotional state had made me weak, but as soon as I went out into the cooling August evening the alcohol went to my head and I suddenly felt light, and the blood surged through me and I could almost forget about Aria.

My next stop was Mother MacCree's. Mostly a college crowd, but I was feeling so good by then that some of the guys at the bar took a liking to me—they were watching baseball and I cheered for whatever team they cheered for so they assumed I was one of them and included me in their rounds of shots. The shots tasted like sour apple and I had two or three and washed them down with a pint. Then I bought a round and the guys all cheered and someone offered me a chicken wing. After that the evening got fuzzier.

At some point I got into someone's car, and then we were someplace else and the other guys were gone but someone new was there, a well-dressed guy with a couple of beautiful women, and he was telling me that he had made millions of dollars selling water filters, and that I looked like I could use some money so if I wanted to know the secret he could tell me about it. I said I'd love to know the secret and in fact had always wanted to be a water filtration salesman. One of the women said I was cute. Then we got into a limo and went to a club down by the water. There was dancing and more drinking, and then the man told me that he was willing to take a chance on me; he felt I had what it took to succeed in the world of water filtration systems. I listened intently as he bought round after round. He had a huge wallet filled with credit cards, which he made a big deal of pulling out and scanning each time he paid for the drinks. Then he offered me a ride home and said that there was a private, invite-only orientation meeting in a few days, and that if I wanted to get started selling water filtration systems, that all it would require was a tiny initial investment of five thousand dollars, and within six months I'd be as rich as him, but when we reached my rooming-house, the woman who said I was cute yelled, "*This* is where you live?" and I got the feeling I wasn't so cute anymore, or such a good prospect for selling water filters, so I got out and the car turned around and got out of there quick and I stumbled upstairs and passed out.

I thought it was all a dream but in the morning I saw the card on the floor: *Mark Polack, American Patriot Water Filtration Systems, Inc.* A logo of an eagle holding what looked like a bomb but was probably a water filter. A corporate address in Jacksonville, Florida. A real class outfit.

My cellphone started buzzing. I checked the screen. It was Aria. I hit the dismiss button. Alerts pinged and blinked at me: I had 10 new voicemails and 20 new text messages. I knew without looking that they were all from her. I had no interest in what she had to say. I turned the phone completely off and put it in the top drawer of my dresser and felt better immediately.

It was ten a.m. I was starving. All that talk about water filtration systems had made me hungry. I dragged myself across the hall and into the shower, then got myself together enough to walk down to the deli. I ordered ham and eggs on a roll, two large coffees with milk, and grabbed a pint of Tropicana. While I was waiting for the sandwich I saw the cover of the *News*: PHOWL PLAY. The *Post* ran a different story on the cover, but along the bottom there was a banner that read, DEAD HEAD: HIPPIE ROCKER SHOCKER AT LI PARK. I took one of each and added them to my order.

"I didn't know you could read, Shambles."

Two cops were standing to my left. I knew the one who'd spoken. It was my old nemesis, Arnie O'Toole. He'd been the closest thing to a school bully that I had to endure at Mumfrey High, which was strange because we came from similar backgrounds: single mothers, financial struggles, the whole sad package. I might have turned out to have been as big a jerk as he was, except I was an only child. He had three older brothers and a sister or two floating around. I'd heard his brothers used to beat the crap out of him, something I luckily avoided growing up. It warped Arnie enough that he started picking on other kids to get his frustration out; eventually he went on to become a cop. I only knew that because my mom tells me everything that goes on in town, especially about my former classmates. It didn't look like he'd gotten any nicer since high school.

"Hey Arnie," I said.

"It's Officer O'Toole, Shambles."

"Okay."

"What's that? You getting wise?"

Arnie's partner shifted uncomfortably but didn't say anything. I knew how their kind liked to stick together.

"I just said okay. Like, okay, I understand."

"Good. I know all about your little adventure, Shambles. You think you're really hot now that you were in the papers and on TV and stuff."

If he'd let me answer I would have told him that it was one of the worst things that had ever happened to me and that if I could go back and do it all differently I would, but he didn't give me the chance.

"I want you to know I don't buy it for a second. Bet you think you're a real hero now."

"No, just lucky."

"That's right. Lucky. The whole thing stinks. You belong with the rest of the perps."

The counter man came over with my sandwich and bagged the order. I paid for everything and took the bag and newspapers and got out of there. Arnie called after me.

"Next time you won't get away so easy!"

I didn't know what he was talking about and I didn't want to. It was like my hangover had become real. A guy like him should be rounding up all the water-filtration salesmen and running the scammers out of town, but no. That's what I meant about being in the spotlight. Once you get into the news, everyone has an opinion about you. It's like you stop being a person and suddenly become a thing, like a soccer ball. Most people just want to toss you around for a bit of fun before moving on, but some people see a soccer ball and feel the overwhelming urge to kick it as hard as they can and keep kicking it and then pull out something sharp and deflated it so nobody could ever have fun with it again. Arnie was definitely one of those people. He hadn't changed a bit since high school, which was fine by me. But he hadn't carried a gun in high school, either.

I got home, lay on my cot and read the story. There wasn't much that I didn't already know, except for one small additional item, running as a sidebar in the *News*:

Source: Shocked Rocker
Victim of Tampered Amp

According to an anonymous source, the shock that killed hippie rocker Gavin Burns might have been due to sabotage. But at least one member of the band's entourage disagreed.

"We checked everything," said "Lizard," the beefy head of the Maine biker gang, Electric Wheels, who accompanied the band on their recent tour. "We set everything up, the band did soundcheck, no problems. If something had happened we'd have known about it."

A police spokesperson had no comment, saying the incident was still under investigation.

I thought about the leader of the biker gang, Lizard, and how he'd told Brent to shut up when we were in the bus. And I wondered what Brent had been trying to tell us when we were interrupted. Maybe it was important, maybe not. It was too much to think about. I went through the DVDs from the library. I decided to watch *Willow*. Might as well enjoy Aria's gifts while I still had them, until she had one of her big brothers come by and make me give it all back. I looked at my cast and felt a twinge of regret. I'd forgotten my appointment, but she had remembered. She'd even gotten me a gift to commemorate the day. Then chosen that day to dump me. It was just as well that I was rid of her.

My mind drifted to Scarlet. She was a free spirit, very different from Aria. She was also older, more experienced. Maybe that's what I needed, someone mature and somewhat stable—someone truly grown-up, rather than someone just pretending to be. Scarlet and I would be spending many hours together, going through her dad's stuff, listing things online, and getting ready for a garage sale. We'd have plenty of time to get to know each other, share secrets, build trust and friendship. She'd teach me the wild ways of hippie love. I bet we'd do it in a tent.

I gave a final look at the picture of Aria, in her white bikini, then put it in the dresser drawer, next to the cellphone. Time to let an older woman indoctrinate me in the mysteries of hippie love under the stars.

The DVD previews were over, and the main menu appeared. I pressed play and settled in to watch *Willow*. My mind kept drifting back to Scarlet, dreaming of the moment when Scarlet and I would start our romance. I had a debate with myself. A part of me said that there was no rush, that I could take my time and let my sorrow about Aria subside a bit. The other side told me that the healthiest thing to do would be to jump on Scarlet the next time I saw her. It didn't take Dr. K to tell me which side would probably win.

CHAPTER 7: I'M OK, YOU'RE DR. K

When the movie was over I got ready to go to my appointment. I was locking the door to my room when Aku appeared in the hallway. And by appear I mean just that—the dude doesn't really enter a place. You turn around and he's just there, and then you blink and he's gone. He usually announces himself with a little throat-clearing sound, which is what he did now.

"Can I ask your opinion on something?"

"Sure."

"Tell me if you see anything."

Aku closed his eyes and mumbled some kind of spell. He waved his hands around. Then he opened his eyes wide and his hands snapped and there was a great burst of flame. I jumped back.

"Holy crap!"

"I'm sorry for startling you. I find the element of surprise is always best in these situations."

"It worked. You almost gave me a heart attack. What's the deal?"

"I'm practicing for the 4-D party tonight. I'm on the potions committee again. Every year my fellow wizards and I try adding something new to the proceedings." He waved his hands again and another fireball flared and disappeared.

"Ahh! Stop!"

"My apologies. What I wanted to know is, does it look real?"

"Real enough to burn my eyebrows off."

"Good. I don't want people to see how I do it."

Aku extended his arm from the end of the robe and turned his hand over. Tucked into his palm was a small metal device.

"It's called a finger flasher. As its name implies, it's used to ignite flash paper."

He revealed his other hand. Small square sheets of paper were attached to his wrist with a rubber band.

"Nitrocellulose. Used by magicians and other conjurers to dazzle and amaze people."

"Why can't you just cast a fire spell, like Gandalf?"

"That's not quite accurate, I'm afraid. Real wizards must rely on a combination of magic and illusion. Would you like to try?"

"Sure."

He handed me the little metal thing. "You slip this around a finger, then create a spark by pressing this. It's basically a flint, if you ever had to make a fire in Boy Scouts."

I practiced with the finger flasher a few times. Aku handed me a sheet of paper.

"If you hold it like so, nobody can see the paper. Then as you wave your hands to cast your spell, the sound of your voice should cover the sound of the device striking. With a bit of practice—there!"

A flash went up in my hands. I could smell the unmistakable odor of burnt arm hair.

"Good! I think you're a natural."

I did it a few more times, then handed the flasher back.

"That's pretty cool."

"Would you like one? I've got several. I'll be happy to lend you one."

"Seriously?"

"Of course. I'm always willing to initiate a fellow traveler into the mystical arts."

"It might come in handy if I ever need to repel a dragon."

"Hmm, doubtful. Being of the fire element themselves, most dragons would not be fooled. But it's very effective against goblins and trolls."

"Good to know."

I started for the stairs then thought of a question.

"What party did you say you were going to?"

I turned around but he was already gone.

Cherry Blossom Drive is located in a nondescript little part of Mumfrey that's pretty much the same as every part of Mumfrey, and can be described with words like cute, quaint, quiet, leafy, sleepy, neat, trim, mowed, clipped, sad, lonely, miserable, isolated, alcoholic and insane. Number 72 is a neat, trim, quaint, cute little house, yellow and blue and white. I parked in front and went up the path to the side door, where a cute and quaint little brass plaque read

Marvin P. Kornbluth, Ph.D., MSW
Family and Couples Counseling
Anger Management

I wasn't there for family or couples counseling, let's put it that way. I had started seeing Dr. K under a judge's order, because of some trouble I got into in the city for defending a woman I loved. The situation got a bit out of hand and I got into quite a bit of trouble as a result. To make matters worse, my probation officer started dating my ex-girlfriend, and I said a silent prayer every day that she was torturing him in the way I knew she was capable of. Some people are brilliant at singing, or cooking, or playing cards; Devil Girl was a master of emotional manipulation and romantic drama. I was no longer obligated to see Dr. K, but between Devil Girl, Aria, and all the crazy stuff that had happened over the summer, I started checking back in with him.

I pushed my way in and a little bell jingled. I sat in the waiting room and looked for something to read. I found a paperback book lying on a copy of *People* that was two months out of date and which I'd already read. I saw Dr. K's name on the cover of the book. The title was *No 'Vorce For Wear: How Children of Divorce Can Thrive and Succeed in Today's World.* My heart got a little heavier.

I wasn't the only child of divorce in the world, but my dad had left when I was small and then just dropped off the face of the earth. I didn't remember him except for some photographs and stories from my mom.

"Sorry to keep you waiting. Please, come in."

Dr. K's voice is so gentle and friendly that it always shocks me. I walked into the office and took my usual chair. His curly brown hair was always a bit too long and messy; he wore open-toed sandals and jeans and a white shirt with a button-down collar. It made me feel good to look at him, as dorky as he was.

He tapped a thick pile of papers on his desk. I recognized the smudged ink as being from my old Royal typewriter.

"I read your account of what happened over the summer, with the golfer. It's quite fascinating."

"Is that good or bad? Am I crazy? Do I need help?"

"It's good. And no, you're not crazy. As for help, everybody needs help in some way, at some point in their lives. But if you're asking whether I think you have more serious problems, at least based on your account of what happened, the answer is no."

He gestured to my lap.

"Did you see anything interesting in my book?"

It was only then that I realized I was still holding *No 'Vorce For Wear.* I handed it to him.

"Sorry."

"I'd loan it to you but it's my only copy at the moment. I'm waiting for more from my publisher."

"What does the title mean? I don't get it."

"It's a play on the expression 'no worse for wear.' I substituted 'vorce, as in 'divorce'. My premise is that kids who live through a divorce can still be 'no worse for wear,' meaning as good as a kid from a two-parent home. What do you think?"

"Honestly?"

"Of course."

"The idea for the book is cool, but I think that's probably the worst title I've ever heard in my life. No offense."

"None taken. What would you suggest?"

"How about, '*May The 'Vorce Be With You*'?"

He smiled. "That's not bad. Maybe a little too Hollywood, but you're definitely creative. I'll go back to the drawing board. You didn't come here to critique my book, did you?"

"No."

He looked at his pad. "The last time you were here we talked about the young lady you're seeing, the one who's now in California."

"Aria."

"How are things going?"

"We broke up."

"What happened?"

"She dumped me for a guy with a boat."

"I'm very sorry to hear that. She seemed like a refreshing change after your last girlfriend, the one who got you into all that trouble."

"Devil Girl."

"You still won't use her real name?"

"Never."

"You know, people let each other down sometimes. Perhaps even most of the time. It's really not within our control."

"I don't have to like it, do I?"

"Of course not. Just as long as you don't let it take over. We can learn ways of letting things go."

"But if I let things go, how will I be able to stay mad?"

"You won't. That's the point."

"Sounds crazy to me, but I'd be willing to try. What's the secret?"

"Have you tried forgiveness?"

"Why should I forgive? I'm not the one with the boat."

"Okay, let's talk about that. Why do you think Aria dumped you for a guy with a boat? Is that all she cares about?"

"In a way. She sends me presents, but that's not my idea of love."

"Of course not. It can be a sign that someone has intimacy issues, or it can simply mean that someone is thinking about us. Some people have trouble trusting, so they use material things instead. Maybe she uses gifts because that's the way she learned how to express her feelings. Do you see what I mean?"

"I guess so."

"Not that it's important, but did you ever send her anything?"

"Yes. I mailed her a set of keys to my place."

Dr. K sat upright, his eyes widened.

"Really? I'm very impressed. Sending someone keys is a very intimate gesture, a sign of genuine trust. It's also a symbol that you're giving someone the literal keys to your heart, your home, your most personal self. Do you feel that's why you did it?"

"To be honest, I just wanted her to have a set in case I lost mine. I figured she could always overnight them to me."

"I see." Dr. K looked at his pad and scribbled furiously. I hate it when he does that.

"The thing is, I met someone else. I only just met her, and she's a bit older, but she seems really cool."

"That's good, that's healthy. You're young, you should be dating. The number one problem I see in my practice is that people commit too quickly. They meet on a Friday and by Monday they're attached at the hip. We've lost the art of playing the field. I don't mean just sex, either, I'm talking about investing the time to get to know someone before latching on for dear life. Ironically, I think people get committed more quickly these days because they figure they can always get divorced if it doesn't work. That's a big part of my book. So who's this other woman, and how old is she?"

"She's a blonde hippie, pushing forty."

"Sounds sexy. When are you going to see her?"

"After I leave here."

"Have you two been intimate yet?"

"No, but I think I'm going to make a move when I go over there. I have this idea that I really want to do it in a tent."

Dr. K laughed. "That's good. Have experiences, don't settle for one idea about how things have to be. Stay open and flexible. And for your information, making love in a tent is fabulous."

"I knew it."

At the end of the session I wrote Dr. K a check and we scheduled another appointment in two weeks. When I left his office I didn't have any clearer idea of who I was or what I was doing, but I always felt a little better.

I decided to swing by the library before going to Scarlet's. There was a wait for one of the computers so

I looked at all the newspapers for any more information about Gavin. *Newsday* had an obituary that focused more on the band's history and had a few extra pictures and CD covers, but no more information about what caused the short circuit. I found myself checking each picture carefully, in case there was one with Scarlet in it. Anything to get my mind off Aria and that bikini.

CHAPTER 8: RETURN OF THE NOT THIN MAN

I got to Scarlet's house around 5 o'clock. She greeted me with the same big smile, except there was something automatic about it now; her eyes didn't sparkle as brightly as they had before.

"How are you feeling?" I asked.

"I've been better."

"Yeah, me too."

We went into the family room. There were several empty cardboard boxes, some packing tape and Sharpie markers.

"Where should we start?"

"I don't know. I know I said we should get started but I'm just too bummed. Why don't we just sit and talk for a while?"

"Sounds good."

We sat on the sectional that took up most of the room. It was unbelievably comfortable. There were different pillows and blankets here and there. It was deeper than my bed was wide; it could have slept six adults comfortably. My mind immediately raced with the possibility of taking Scarlet right then and there, on that big luxurious upholstery. I sat down and she sat next to me, her thigh touching mine. Then she leaned over and put her head on my shoulder. Tears rolled silently down her cheeks.

I put my arm around her. My first thought was to comfort her, but I couldn't ignore my desire for her. I was glad that she felt comfortable enough with me to open up with her feelings. Maybe someday I could feel the same way with her. I felt like I had a few years' worth of tears built up inside me, just waiting to come out. Then she pulled herself back and reached for a tissue from the box on the table.

"I'm sorry. I've been like this all day. I just can't get over it."

She reached over and slipped her hand in mine. I squeezed gently and she squeezed back. She looked at me with her tear-streaked face.

"I don't believe in accidents," she said. "I believe that I was meant to run into you at the library. I can't tell you how good it feels to have you here."

My heart was pounding. Was this the right time to make a move? What would Dr. K say about it? I'd just been rejected by Aria. Being rejected a second time in less than twenty-four hours would be too much for me to handle. If I was misreading the situation then it could do more harm than good. There was no harm in waiting and being sure. I tried thinking of an innocent topic.

"Did you tell China about what happened?"

"Of course. She was freaked out, but she doesn't know those guys like I do. She only met them a handful of times, so it hasn't hit her as hard."

Scarlet reclined a bit on the couch, and positioned her body so she was facing me. She brought one leg up and rested her knee on my thigh. *Kiss her*, half of me yelled. *Not yet*, the other side shouted back. My heart thumped so loudly in my chest that I was sure she could hear it.

"At the library you said she was working on a movie."

"Not exactly. She's doing a series of instructional yoga videos. It's a really cool idea. I'm helping her produce them, and I'm one of the featured students." She pressed her palms together and straightened her spine. "*Ommmm*. It's so much fun."

The thought of Scarlet in a sexy little outfit, stretching this way and that, was almost too much for me to bear. I was already hot and bothered but I suddenly got much hotter and bothered-er.

"I can't wait to see those," I said hoarsely. Scarlet wrinkled her nose at me.

"I don't think you'll like them."

"Why not?"

"The series is called *Yoga for Lesbians*."

My stomach dropped. My voice cracked. "Really?"

"Yeah, sorry to say. There's going to be a bunch of them: *Yoga for the Pregnant Lesbian, Yoga for the Vegan Lesbian, Yoga for the Married Lesbian*, and so on. It's going to be like those *Chicken Soup* books, except with video."

"And lesbians," I said sadly.

"Right! I knew you'd totally get it! Except—wait, that's my phone."

Scarlet's phone was buzzing on the coffee table. She picked it up and answered, then got up and walked into the front room.

Sure, I got it. There went my romantic dreams, my vision of our own personal little Woodstock, of painting each other's naked bodies with edible paint and listening to the Grateful Dead while feeding our pet butterflies.

The Shambles' Curse had struck again. The only women who wanted me were heartless manipulators who enjoyed breaking my heart. I finally met a beautiful, sane woman who could teach me the erotic secrets of hippie love, and she was a lesbian. Of course. No wonder she was so close and friendly with me—I was her buddy, her garage sale partner, her employee. I decided not to think or speak of it again. Scarlet came back into the room.

"That was Brent. He said he couldn't talk in the bus yesterday but that he wants to talk to me tonight. He said he might know something about Gavin's death."

"Like what?"

"He couldn't say; it wasn't safe to talk. I asked him to text me but he said he didn't want to leave any record, in case our communications were being monitored."

"Seriously?"

"Crazy, right? I'm as paranoid as the next person when it comes to government surveillance, but that sounds overboard to me."

"Where are you meeting him?"

"He'll be at the 4-D party tonight."

"My neighbor Aku said something about that. What's a forty party? Does everyone bring big bottles of beer?"

"Not *forty*, *4-D*. The four D's stand for Deadheads, Druids, and Dungeons & Dragons. Once a year they get together for a party. There used to be big enough scenes to support each group individually, but as their numbers have shrunk over the years they've had to combine."

"These are tough times to be a nerd."

"You said it. Speaking of nerds, I was kind of hoping you'd go with me. China's supposed to be going too but she's been kind of flaky lately. Brent said to meet him there around eight."

"That reminds me. I saw something in the paper today. An anonymous source claimed that what happened to Gavin might not have been an accident. Do you think that's what he's talking about?"

"I don't know. They're always going to say something like that, to make it sound sensational. Most likely someone wasn't paying attention. If there was any negligence involved then I hope they find out who it was and punish them. I have a feeling I might know what Brent wants to see me about."

"What?"

"Nothing. Just personal stuff."

I thought back to what the big biker, Lizard, had said to Scarlet when he saw her: *You have something of ours.* I got a feeling that Scarlet wasn't being completely honest with me. Just like my ex-girlfriend, Devil Girl, and now my ex-girlfriend, Aria. I kept getting hurt by women not being truthful with me. Which would be fine, if only they'd be honest about it. I knew there was a flaw somewhere in my thinking, but I couldn't figure it out.

"Hey, are you all right? You look like you've been through a war."

"I feel like I have."

"Want to tell me about it?"

"It'll probably bore you."

"Right now I'd give my right arm to be bored. Come on into the kitchen, I made some lemonade."

Scarlet led the way. It was a pretty room, brighter and sunnier than the living room, with pale wood cabinets and a recent coat of yellow paint. The counters and table were like out of a classic old diner, polished and gleaming chrome with a faint boomerang pattern on the top. I cheered up just being in there.

Scarlet pulled a pitcher from the fridge and put it on the table, then retrieved a couple of tall glasses from a cabinet and sat across from me. She poured two lemonades and handed me a glass. "I hope you like it."

I took a sip. It was great lemonade. It always amazed me when people were able to do things like that. I didn't have any skills except getting in trouble. I could always count on that.

"So what happened? Why so sad?"

I paused before answering. I wasn't sure if I wanted to go into all the details of my drama with Aria. Then I thought, if Scarlet wanted to have me as her straight friend to do things with, go to concerts and parties when China was busy, then I might as well get her perspective on my own troubles.

"My girlfriend broke up with me yesterday."

"Oh, no. Why?"

I filled her in, being as brief as possible—Aria going to California, sending me gifts, and me being jealous at her financial means and the freedom it gave her. Then I explained about the cable TV, and how I'd forgotten to go to the doctor to get the cast off, and how Aria had told me that she'd met a guy and was on his sailboat. When I finished, Scarlet looked truly sad, which made me feel better.

"That's harsh, dude. Why did she give you cable if she knew she was breaking up with you?"

"I don't know. She probably met the guy after she placed the order. The most ridiculous part was that she accused me of being on a date with you."

"Why? Because we went to the Phestival together?"

"Yeah. She acted like it was a huge betrayal. When really she was just looking for an excuse to make herself feel better about dumping me."

Scarlet nodded. "Could be. We gals can be complicated sometimes. But personally I think she's nuts for dumping such a great guy. Any woman would be lucky to have you for a boyfriend."

I smiled weakly then took another sip of lemonade.

"What's the rest of the band going to do now?"

"I don't know. Probably just go back to Bangor and become full-time potheads."

"What if the story in the paper is right? Who'd want to do something like that to Gavin?"

"Nobody that I know of."

"What about those bikers? They seem like a rough bunch."

A shadow crossed her face. She shook her head and it went away. "I doubt it. I mean, those guys are trouble, don't get me wrong, but to do something like that? When they're touring with the band, and part of the set-up crew and all? They'd be the most likely suspects, and they're responsible for the equipment, so why would they do something that they'd almost certainly be blamed for?"

"What if they thought they could make it look like an accident, and someone found out about it and decided to tell the press? And why was Lizard so quick to tell Brent to shut up? It sounded like a threat to me."

"That's just the way he is with everybody. Real big shot, likes to control everyone around him. I wouldn't read too much into it. You start thinking that way too much, and everybody looks guilty after a while."

"I still don't trust that memorabilia guy, Martin. He's up to no good."

Scarlet looked off into the distance, behind me. "Speak of the devil."

I turned. There, peeking over the curtain, were a pair of beady eyes attached to a somewhat fat and greasy-looking forehead. We were being watched.

CHAPTER 9: THE TRIP

The beady eyes fixed on Scarlet, then moved over to me. They registered surprise. I stood up.

"Don't worry about him," Scarlet said. "I really think he's harmless."

"Like hell he is," I snarled.

The back door was locked. By the time I fumbled with the latch, then the knob, got the thing opened and then unlocked and unlatched the screen door, got that open, then pushed my way out and got around the side of the house, Martin was already back to his car and starting the engine. I ran down to the street and reached his car just as he pulled away, a dirty little smile on his face. I stood huffing on the blacktop, clenching and unclenching my fists.

Scarlet came out from the side of the house and stood at the top of the driveway.

"Is he gone?"

"Yes," I gasped, out of breath. Those six weeks of doing nothing hadn't helped my conditioning any. The booze I drank the night before didn't help either.

"Are you all right?"

"I think so. Just need to catch my breath."

Scarlet started down the driveway. "You're too young to be so out of shape," she scolded, teasing me. "You should take one of China's yoga classes."

"Do I look like a pregnant lesbian to you?"

"Um, can I refuse to answer that?"

I was about to say something when I heard a roar. I turned and saw a car zoom over the crest of the hill.

Behind the wheel, I saw the sweaty, crazed face of the memorabilia dealer. He was heading right for me.

"Look out!"

I jumped out of the way and dove onto the front lawn as the front right tire of the car bounced up onto the curb, missing my legs by inches. If I'd been standing another three feet out in the road I'd have been street meat.

The car scraped off the curb again with a sickening crunch, and the tires squealed as the car turned sharply around the cul-de-sac and sped away.

"Are you all right?"

"I landed on my arm. I need help."

She ran to my side and helped me roll over. It had broken my fall. I felt a fair amount of pain, but I couldn't tell if it was more from fear or the injury.

"I have to get this thing off," I said.

"Shouldn't you go to the hospital?"

"I can't deal with sitting around there for hours, explaining everything. I was supposed to have it taken off already anyway."

"I've actually removed a cast once before, up in Maine. Do you want me to try?"

"You have something you can use?"

"A Dremel tool. I'm sure I've got the right bit. Do you want me to call the police?"

"No. I have my own issues with them. I really don't want them involved."

"That's cool with me, I'm no fan of the cops either. But are you sure you're all right?"

"Yeah. My arm hurts, but I don't think it's re-broken or anything."

"Come on into the back. I'll get the tools."

We went to the backyard. Scarlet offered me a lounge chair and then brought out our lemonade. Then she brought out a hand tool and a towel. She stuffed the towel between the opening in the cast and my arm.

"Just rest your arm. I'll be very careful."

I watched as she worked. She had a gentle touch and a steady hand. In a few minutes it was off. I rubbed it, moved my hand around.

"How's it feel?"

"Great. A little weak, but this is a huge improvement. Thank you."

"It's the least I can do for a hometown hero." She picked up the pieces of the cast and frowned. "I never got to sign it."

Her phone rang. I could tell by the nature of the conversation that it was a friend in Maine. They were talking about the tragedy with Gavin. When that call ended she had another, then another, as word spread. She was on the phone for most of the next hour, talking to friends back up in Maine, and her brother in Florida.

I lay in the sun, enjoying the feeling of the warmth on my arm. The area that had been covered by the cast was all right, but I'd done something to my shoulder when I landed, and my ribs hurt where I fell onto the cast. A sharp, throbbing pain went from my ribcage to my neck.

I needed painkillers. I got up from the lounge chair. Scarlet looked at me and I pointed to my arm. She asked her friend to hold on.

"Sorry to interrupt. Do you have any aspirin?"

"Oh, sure. Right over the sink." She motioned to the back door. Then she went back to talking.

I went inside and opened the cabinet over the kitchen sink. There were only mugs and a few drinking glasses in there. I didn't see any aspirin. They I spied a small clay pot with a lid. I took down the clay pot and looked inside. Bingo. The familiar white tablets with the cross on the front. I was very familiar with them. I popped four, washed then down with some water from the sink and went back out. Scarlet was just getting off the phone.

"Sorry about that, that was one of my old friends from Maine. She said everyone up there is freaking out about Gavin. I'll probably go up there for the service, or whatever they end up having. You find what you were looking for okay?"

"Fine, thanks."

The phone rang again. Scarlet looked at the display window.

"I better get this. Sorry."

Scarlet answered and started telling the story again. I settled back in the lounge chair and let the sun hit my face. It felt good. But like everything else, the sun would set and the day would be over. Maybe the secret to life was understanding that the good stuff didn't last, so you had to grab it while you could. In the past weeks I'd been beaten up, chased, shot, almost strangled, and accused of a bunch of crimes that could have sent me away for life. And yet here I was, lying in the sun in a backyard with a beautiful blonde. Okay, so she was a lesbian. You couldn't have everything. At that moment I realized I had more than enough.

"What is he still doing here?"

I looked up from my daydream and saw China standing by the back door. She made a wide-eyed face at Scarlet and jerked her thumb in my direction. Scarlet waved her off and continued her conversation. After a few seconds, China turned around and went back inside, slamming the kitchen door behind her. Scarlet told the caller that she had to go, then she clicked the button and looked at me.

"What's wrong with Chi?"

"Beats me."

"How's your arm feeling?"

"Good. Really good, in fact."

"Great! I'm going to see what's eating Chi. You need anything?"

"I'm beautiful, baby."

Scarlet gave me a funny look, then she went into the house. I lifted my arm and looked at it. When it moved there seemed to be a trail of light behind it, like a neon tracing of my arm. It was very strange and quite beautiful. I moved my hand through the air. The colors intensified. My hand and arm now looked like they were made of rubber. Every motion was bending, drooping, throbbing. I lifted my other arm. Same thing.

I suddenly felt a rush up my back, like a million microscopic hamsters all running up my spinal cord at the same time. It was intense, and felt really good. I leaned back in the lounge chair and arched my back and moaned. The sound in my chest and throat was like a fog horn, bellowing deep into the night.

"Bert? Are you okay? Is everything all right?"

China and Scarlet had come back outside. Scarlet was looking at me with a funny expression. She glowed like irradiated neon butter.

"Everything is fan-freaking-*tastic*," I sighed, sinking lower into the chair. The sun sparkled off my skin like that vampire guy in *Twilight*. I lifted my arms and looked at the twinkling display in wonder. It was beautiful!

Scarlet came to my side and stood over the chair, frowning.

"What's happening? You're acting strangely all of a sudden."

"Could you please move?" I asked her, dreamily. "You're blocking my sparkles."

"Sparkles?" Her voice sounded far away, like it was echoing under water.

China scrunched her nose at me. "Are you high or something? Scar, what did you give him?"

"Nothing! I just told Bert where the Tylenol was."

"And I found it," I purred. "In that groovy clay pot over the kitchen sink."

"Kitchen sink?" Scarlet thought for a moment. "Oh no." She turned and ran back into the house. A minute later she came back out, holding the little clay pot in her hand.

"Is this what you mean? Is this the clay pot you're talking about?"

"Sure, baby. It was right where you told me it would be."

"I meant the *bathroom* sink, not the kitchen! The medicine cabinet! I just assumed you knew what I meant!"

"It's okay," I said. "My arm feels fine. All three of them, in fact."

Scarlet crouched by my side and put her hand on my chest. The million microscopic hamsters rolled over under her touch and started giggling. My whole body shook from the energy of her touch.

"The spirit guardians are strong in you," I moaned.

China had gone from snotty to smiling. She was enjoying herself now.

"Is that what I think it is?" she smiled. "Oh man, you've really done it now."

Scarlet shushed her, then turned back to me and spoke sweetly. "Look, Bert, I don't know how to tell you this, but what you took wasn't aspirin. It's an experimental drug that my friend came up with. Ex-friend, I should say."

"Far out."

"How did you know?"

"Know what?"

"The name."

"What name?"

"The drug. It's called Far Out."

"Like I said. Far out."

"Forget it, Scar. He's totally flying."

Scarlet continued speaking in that sweet, gentle way of hers, except now it sounded like there was a robot in an echo chamber trapped somewhere in her diaphragm.

"How many did you take? (*take take take*) Please don't tell me you took two (*two two two*)," her voice echoed.

"I didn't," I crooned back.

"Thank goodness."

"I took four."

"What?!"

"Oh, man," China snorted. "Better tie him down or he's gonna be in orbit pretty soon."

"This is serious, Chi! We don't know what might happen. He might have to go to the hospital and get his stomach pumped!"

"No hospital," I said. "Besides, I'm already pumped." I tried to make a muscle but the middle fell out of my bicep. It drooped and swung back and forth like in a cartoon. I fell back onto the chair and started laughing hysterically.

"I just wish I knew what the safe limit is," Scarlet said. "I'd call Pete and ask him, since he made the stuff, but after what happened between us I can't."

I wrapped my arms around myself and rolled off the lounge chair onto the grass, face down. I spread my arms and breathed deeply. The grass tickled my face, the earth below smelled heavenly, the earthworms came out of their holes to see what was happening. A millipede in a top hat and wearing hundreds of tiny sneakers peeked out from under a leaf.

"Hello, earthworms," I said. "I'm hugging the world."

Scarlet rubbed my back. "I'm going to explain it a little to you, hon, so you don't worry, so you understand what's going on. Okay?"

I rolled over onto my back. Scarlet's hair flowed and vibrated like rivers of gold.

"I'm not worried. A man who hugs the world has nothing to fear. And don't call me Bert. From now on, call me Pee-Wee von Sprinkle-sparks."

China howled with laughter at this. Scarlet ignored her.

"What you took is an experimental drug, made by a guy I knew up in Maine. He's a brilliant chemist and makes these amazing psychedelic drugs, really cutting-edge stuff. Do you understand me so far?"

"Loud and clear, Goldenrod Space Chicken."

"Far Out is designed to have three distinct parts. They're time-released, and each part is different."

"Just like *21 Jump Street*," I said.

"Yes, but this came first. Anyway, you're on the first part of the trip right now. The first part is kind of like Ecstasy, you'll feel really happy and good for a while, with some hallucinations. Then next part is like LSD, and it should be less touchy-feely and more intellectual and philosophical. Plus, you'll get more intense visuals—swirly colors and visions, stuff like that."

"But I'm already getting that kind of stuff," I said. "Can't you see my skin sparkling? Can't you see the beautiful purple grass and orange sky?"

"Maybe the LSD part comes first and then the Ecstasy," Scarlet said. "I don't remember now."

"It's probably because he took so much," China said. "It's overloading his system."

"We should take him to the hospital."

"And do what? Tell them what happened? Give them the drugs, so they can analyze them? Tell them where you got them? Do you really want to go to jail?"

"Don't be dramatic, Chi."

"Dramatic? Are you kidding me? They'll have cops, DEA, SWAT teams, helicopters on you in no time. You know how these fascist cowboys love acting like big shots. Don't forget they can probably take your whole house and everything in it, no questions asked, thanks to our wonderful war on drugs."

"I'd rather risk that than have him die of an overdose!"

"He's not going to die, for God's sake. Don't be dramatic. Didn't you tell me that one of your friends took a tablet every hour for like twelve hours?"

"Yeah, and he's still wandering around Bangor, asking people where his teddy bear is."

"So how long does it last?" I asked.

"About two hours."

"That's not so bad. We'll just hang here until it's over."

"No, I mean two hours for each part of the trip, not total. The total time is about six to eight hours. But who knows, it might be longer because you took so much. It'll certainly be more intense."

"We were supposed to go to the party tonight, remember?" China asked. "Do you really want to babysit another eight hours of this?"

"The party's not going to happen. At least not until I get Bert to a safe place. This is my responsibility. I can't leave him."

"All right, I'm heading home. This isn't my scene. Try playing him some music, that usually helps." China turned to me. "I bet you're into that sad country-western stuff, about how she done you wrong."

"Actually, I kind of like show tunes and old disco."

"You're weird. Good luck, Scar."

"Hey, China," I said. She turned and looked at me. "What?"

"That video series you're doing, the *Yoga for Lesbians* thing?"

"What about it?"

"I've been meaning to ask you about it. I can't figure it out. Is yoga really different for lesbians? I thought yoga was just yoga."

China gave me a look and shook her head.

"Typical man."

Scarlet put her arm around China.

"Come on, hon, I'll walk you out."

They walked around the side of the house, to the front. Right then I realized something: I was having fun—real fun, for the first time in years. I was a young man, hanging out with two old hippie lesbians, tripping my face off on a powerful experimental drug that might cause permanent brain damage. It was everything a guy my age should be doing. I was suddenly filled with a tremendous sense of peace and calm. When Scarlet came back a minute later I sat upright on the grass.

"I'm going," I said.

"Where, the hospital?"

"No, to the 4-D party."

"I don't think that's a good idea."

"You said there will be Deadheads there. You think I'm going to be the only person there who's flying?"

"Good point. It's probably the safest place you could be right now." She looked at me skeptically. "You really sure you're up for this?"

"I haven't felt this good in years."

"I don't know if that's more of a commentary on my friend's drug-making skills, or a sign of how unhappy your life has been."

"A little of both."

She thought for a moment, shrugged and then sighed.

"What the heck. If nothing else you'll probably be the life of the party."

CHAPTER 10: LIFE BEGINS AT 4-D

We pulled up to the Knights of Columbus Hall a little before eight. It was a plain brick building, near the end of a long dark street that ran parallel to the railroad tracks. The lights were on inside and there were some colorful-looking characters milling around the front. Scarlet found a spot, turned off the engine and put her hand on my arm.

"Remember, you have some control over the experience. Maybe not much, considering you took four, but if you start to freak out just keep telling yourself that it's not real, that everything is going to be all right. I'll try to stick by you but if we get separated I want you to find me, and I'll take care of you."

"You got it, Apple Starlight Dumpling."

There was an admission fee, five or ten dollars. Scarlet paid. I was in no condition to find my pockets, let alone make a transaction. The bills fluttered and unfurled like leaves falling from the tree of life. As the man handed Scarlet her change, I looked more closely. George Washington winked at me. We got stamps on our hands and we went in.

Along the wall to my left, tables were set up with chairs around them, where people were intensely involved playing games. I assumed they were the Dungeons & Dragons crowd. Dice rolled, maps and charts were consulted, and the vibe was very tense and competitive.

To the right of me, it looked more like a high school science fair, with things bubbling and guys in robes and wizard hats. I expected to see a clay volcano with baking soda lava flowing down the sides, or a Mentos cannon. Gathered on the opposite side of the room, across from the entrance, were the Deadheads. They were wearing tie-dyed shirts for the most part, which glowed and swirled under the black lights. I couldn't be sure but I could swear that they were dancing even though there was nobody on stage. It might have been the drugs. Speaking of drugs, I noticed that I was able to control the Far Out somewhat, like Scarlet said. I could feel it in me, still buzzing around my blood, but for the moment it felt like the worst might be over.

"Hold on, tiger." Scarlet pulled out her phone and looked at it. "Brent just texted me. He said he's on his way; should be here in ten minutes. That's good. You never know with these musician types; they might keep you waiting for hours."

"I think it's the drummers who do that."

"What should we do in the meantime? Want to go visit the Druids?"

"Sure. Aku should be here."

We walked over to the row of wizards. Most were tending cauldrons; some were laying down cards. One was waving a wand, casting spells. As we approached the line I saw a purple robe with silver stars and moons all over it. Aku turned around and smiled.

"Bert! What a pleasant and entirely unexpected surprise. I didn't think you'd be interested in something like this or else I would have invited you."

"Neither did I. What is all this?"

"You're looking at the remnants of some once-vibrant subcultures, back in the 1970s and 80s. There was a time when Dungeons & Dragons conventions would attract thousands of players. Now most people are into MTG."

"Is that like OMG?"

"No, forgive me for assuming. It stands for *Magic: The Gathering*, a newer, and extremely popular role-playing game that's based on cards rather than dice. As time passes and new ideas take hold, people go their separate ways."

"Like what happened to the Dead after Jerry died," Scarlet added. Aku nodded appreciatively. She stuck out her hand.

"I'm Scarlet. I think I've seen you around before."

"Yes, I believe so. I am Aku the Mystic."

"How do you guys know each other?"

"We both cruise the Spirit Realm for chicks," I said. Aku smiled patiently.

"Actually, Bert and I are neighbors."

"So what are you doing here? Is this your potion?"

Aku stirred the smoky cauldron with a crooked stick.

"Yes. This year I made my special Night Vision potion. It's always quite a hit, but I don't do it every year as the necessary salamander skin can be hard to obtain." He poured some into a small plastic cup and offered it to Scarlet. "One draught of this and you will see as clearly as if it were midday."

"No thanks," she said. "I don't need to see any more weird stuff tonight. I'd rather not be seen at all, in fact."

"Ah. In that case you should see Mandrake, at the next table. He has a Potion of Invisibility. How about you, Bert?" Aku held the cup my way.

"What did you call it? Night Vision potion?" I took the cup. "Why not. Can't be any worse than beer goggles."

I shot it down. It gave a familiar burn in my throat, and had a fruity taste but also some unique flavors I didn't recognize, spicy and kind of earthy.

"Interesting. Needs more bat wing."

Aku smiled. "Or perhaps more vodka."

"That too."

"Speaking of vodka, you don't seem yourself tonight, Bert."

"Far Out," I grinned. Aku looked puzzled.

"It's kind of a long story," Scarlet said. "I'm trying to find a friend of mine. Do you know Brent, from the band Phowl?"

"No, not personally. Bert told me about what happened to the singer, and then I saw it on the news. I was very sad to hear it; I'm sorry for your loss."

"Thank you. What kind of potion did you say your friend had?"

"'Tis an invisibility potion, milady," said the wizard at the next cauldron. He scooped some out and ladled it into a plastic cup. Scarlet took a sip.

"Oooh, that's good. Is there clove in here?"

"If there is, 'tis only the clove of cloven hoof, milady."

"The tequila is a nice touch too," she laughed. She gulped it down, shook her head quickly a few times and smacked her lips. "Really burns going down. Any more of that and I'll be so invisible I'll be unconscious!" We all laughed.

"If I happen to recognize your friend Brent I shall inform him you were looking for him," said Aku. We thanked the wizards and went toward the stage. As we walked away Scarlet looped her arm in mine.

"There's more to you than I realized," she said happily.

"There's more to you too."

"Really?"

"Sure. I mean, I can still see you. So much for that invisibility potion."

"I'm not sure it's supposed to make me *literally* invisible," she laughed. "But it might allow a person to not be seen. I like being an observer, a spy sometimes.

If I could have one superpower it would probably be invisibility. What would your superpower be?"

"I'd be rich."

"I never considered that a superpower before, but who knows?" Scarlet felt her pocket. "Wait a sec. I think Brent just texted me again."

Scarlet pulled the phone from her tight cut-offs. She flicked her thumb a few times.

"He wants me to meet him by the back door. He said to be sure I'm alone. Man, he's paranoid. I'll see what he has to say and come back and find you. Stay out of trouble."

Someone came up to the mic and announced a musical act. I didn't catch the name. Then a woman came out from the wings, rolling a harp. The Deadheads cheered. She sat down and thanked everyone in a mumbly, fake-sincere and overly gentle voice that made me think she was probably a total nightmare to be around for any length of time. She introduced her first song as being "about a dragon," which I assumed meant an ex-boyfriend.

The music didn't do much for me. My eyes drifted to the D&D players. They fascinated me, and I wasn't exactly sure why. Then it hit me: it was the movie *Willow*. The inspiring story of a little guy who saves a baby girl from an evil queen, with the help of some magic pixies and a wise witch. It dawned on me that movies might not be real, but magic was. So were little people!

I walked over to the game tables in a trance. I was on a quest, though I didn't understand the nature or import of it yet. I couldn't get the huge grin off my face. Each table had six players, mostly in costumes. They were almost all men, but I was pleased to see a few women here and there; it made things seem less weird somehow. Everywhere people were throwing dice, consulting tables and charts, with these maps and figurines on the table. I couldn't take my eyes off the little figures. They seemed alive to my tripping eyes, I could swear some of them were moving and talking. I stopped at one table and bent over. I was right! One of the miniature figures lowered his sword and looked up at me.

"You are not a believer, are you?" he said.

"I wasn't until now," I replied.

He gave a hearty chuckle. "You have courage, human, showing your face in a place such as this. However, I am here to protect you."

"How are you going to do that? You're only an inch tall."

The figure laughed. "I'm a level 22 Ranger with a Flame Tongue. Behold!"

The Ranger extended his arm at an ugly little hunchback creature on the table and a funnel of flame shot out of the end of the sword and turned the creature to a pile of dust.

"Holy shit!" I cried. I looked up at the others at the table. My eyes were bugged out. "Did any of you just see that?"

They did not look amused. One of them spoke up. "Begone, human," he said.

I looked back down at the Ranger. He looked up at me with pleading eyes. "Please, don't leave me with these nerds," he said.

I understood my mission. I grabbed the Ranger off the table. "I will protect thee!" I cried.

"Hey! Give me back Prince Shieldheart!"

"To the Batcave!" I yelled.

With the Ranger in my hand, I ran up to the front of the room, where the Deadheads were swaying gently to the music. This was a whole different scene. I stared at the woman on stage: she had long golden tresses and a ring of white flowers around her head. She was glowing, electric, alive. The strings shimmered and wobbled as she played her electric harp. She wore one of those headset microphones, but when she sang I could barely see her lips move; it was like the music was coming from another place.

I stood, mesmerized. I felt something squirm in my hand. It was Prince Shieldheart. I could hear his muffled cry. "Hey, let me see!" I opened my hand and lifted it up, with the Ranger in my palm. He stood still, watching her in awe. I looked to my right. One of the Deadheads was looking at me, dancing and grinning. He nodded to Prince Shieldheart and laughed. "That's awesome, man, you're letting your little dude friend enjoy the music too." At that moment I decided that I liked Deadheads. Deadheads understood, Deadheads could appreciate beauty. Not like those freaks at the D&D tables.

I leaned over to my newfound friend, the Deadhead. "She's lip-synching," I yelled. He looked at me strangely and shook his head. "She's lip-synching!" I cried louder, so he could hear me.

"No, she's not," he said emphatically. He moved a little away from me and folded his arms.

I turned to Prince Shieldheart. "Did I say something wrong?"

"Apparently so," he replied. "Now still thy tongue so that I may enjoy the musical spell this lass is casting o'er us all."

I felt a heavy finger, which I later found out was because it was sheathed in a chainmail glove, thudding on my shoulder. I turned and saw the player from the table, with two other armored friends behind him.

"Could I please have my figure back?"

I suddenly wondered what I was doing, holding a one-inch high painted metal figurine in my hand, pointed toward a hippie harp player with a voice that sounded kind of like Miss Piggy of the Muppets if she were on heavy anti-depressants.

"Sure," I said. "Sorry about that." I rotated carefully to present Prince Shieldheart back to his rightful owner. Just then one of the swaying, dancing Deadheads bumped into me. The figure bounced out of my hand and to the ground in the middle of the crowd.

"No!" The D&D player looked horrified. "It took me three days to paint him!"

"I'll get him," I said, but the player pushed past me into the crowd and began shoving the Deadheads out of the way.

"Hey, man, not cool!"

By this time the confrontation had caught the attention of the other D&D players. Several more ran over to see what the commotion was about. I soon learned the hard way that D&D players—at least the hardcore ones, which these guys seemed to be—were sort of like gun nuts: both were looking for any excuse to use their weapons. Swords were drawn. A big, heavily-armored guy with a serious Orc mask on came to the front, his sword pointed at me. I expected a funnel of flame to shoot out and turn me to ashes, but none came.

"You!"

The Orc pulled his mask back. It was the memorabilia dealer who had run into my car.

"This is the fiend who threatened me!" he yelled to his compatriots, who were now drawing their own daggers, maces, pikes and swords. I would have done anything at that moment to have my Leatherman.

"He defiled my chariot then thwarted my attempt to find the missing axe! I'll behead you, monster! Or my name's not Kojo Rigidspine!"

He pushed the point of his sword into me. Lucky for me it was only plastic, but it was still pretty pointy. He lifted the blade as if to strike me.

Suddenly there was a flash of light. It momentarily blinded me. I heard a booming voice behind me. It was Aku, chanting some kind of spell:

By the dragon's might
On this August night
I summon thee
To protect those around me!

At that exact moment the lights went out.

CHAPTER 11: RIOT AT THE NERD FACTORY

There was a big roar of whoops and whoas from the crowd. There was also a lot of laughing, which seemed to be coming mostly from the Deadheads. There was just enough light from the candles, glow sticks, and glow in the dark shirts that some of the Deadheads were wearing to give the place a funhouse atmosphere. The wizards took the opportunity to make some abracadabra stuff happen—poofs and flashes and colored smoke.

The blackout changed everything for me. It was as if the normal, overhead lights of the K of C hall had kept me grounded somewhat in reality, and allowed me to resist the full force of the Far Out. When I saw the colored lights, candles, and bubbling potions of the Druids, all bets were off. The drugs rushed back through my system like some kind of dam bursting, and the sights and sounds became wildly exaggerated. I was no longer at a party, but in a big budget Hollywood blockbuster.

And a big Orc was charging me.

It was Martin. He was slashing his plastic sword, moving closer. I backed up to the stage; then there was nowhere else to go. Martin raised the sword and swung. Suddenly there was a blue flash and the sword deflected to the side, as if repelled by an invisible force field. I looked to my left and saw Aku, his hand extended, a look of such intense concentration on his face like I'd never seen.

The Orc backpedaled a bit.

"The foul human has the protection of a Wizard!" he cried.

I spied something shiny on the ground. I reached between the legs of a hippie and picked it up. It was the figurine. It had been stepped on and crushed. I held up the mangled piece of metal. One of the Orcs saw it and cried out:

"He's killed Prince Shieldheart!"

I felt pretty crushed too. I'd become quite attached to that little fellow.

"I'm sorry!" I cried. "I meant no harm!"

More joined the fray. There was shoving and pushing going on between Orcs and Deadheads. The harpist kept playing, bravely, but without the benefit of amplification.

The other wizard, Mandrake, came up next to Aku. He wove his hands around in the air, them flung them forward, and two more flashes of light appeared. Orcs scurried and cowered, except for a few brave ones.

"It's just flash paper!" one of them yelled.

"Are these costumes flammable?" the one next to him asked.

Martin pulled his mask back on. "Wizards or no," he cried, "they cannot take all of us at once! Attack!"

It was mayhem. The Druids were using their flash paper left and right. One of them lifted a large wooden staff and yelled, "You shall not pass!" A feisty Orc climbed onstage and attempted to harass the harpist, who was having none of it. She saw him in time and skillfully got up from her stool and swung the harp around on its little pointy base and hit him broadside against the temple. The Orc howled and apologized and ran off stage.

Some of the D&D players did not share the communal spirit, and were using the opportunity to settle scores with other players. I saw several separate battles going on. Swords and maces flew through the air. Another group was ganging up on the Deadheads, who weren't fighting anyone. The tie-dyed patterns on their shirts, many of which were glowing in the near darkness, were perfect targets. I saw one player lift a crossbow. I stood frozen in horror as he fired, and saw the projectile hit the swirly center of a Deadhead's chest. The colors pulsated and swirled, and ran down the front of the shirt as the blood joined the other colors in unholy matrimony. But the Deadhead didn't drop. He stood there, grinning stupidly, the arrow stuck straight out of his chest, and I saw the hippie get a demonic look on his face as he pulled the arrow out and looked at it.

"Dude, is that a Nerf crossbow?" he asked.

"Verily," replied the player. "I need that back, by the way." He took back the Velcro-tipped projectile, reloaded and took aim at another tie-dyed shirt. This time it was Scarlet. She put up her hand and glared at the guy.

"Dude, if you shoot me with that thing I'm going to shove it down your mutton-hole."

The player lowered the crossbow sheepishly, just as a fat dwarf in chainmail came up behind him and hit him with one of those Thor hammers you can get at the drug store around Halloween. I saw a number of dazed hippies with Nerf darts stuck all over them.

"Bert, we have to get out of here!"

The lights came back on, momentarily disorienting the crowd. Scarlet took my hand and pulled me across the floor. We saw a lighted emergency exit. It whooped and howled as we pushed through.

We spilled out into the still night air. It smelled sweet and good. Suddenly, I felt a new wave of wonderful feeling wash over me; something new and indescribable was happening. Scarlet had walked ahead. She turned, saw my expression, came back and took me by the arm. As she walked, she radiated a pink glow around her, and my skin tingled like every cell was crying out to be hugged. The touch of her hand on my arm was like a thousand fragrant bubbles filled with warm honey and goose down had exploded under my skin. I shuddered, my eyes rolled back into my head and I moaned.

"Oh, God, don't stop touching me like that," I said.

"Keep moving. We're getting out of here."

"I'm being rescued by the fairest maiden of them all," I sighed dreamily.

"I don't know about that. Besides, you're tripping. What happened back there?"

"I was trying to save Prince Shieldheart. Alas, he was trampled, but I saved him." I held out the squashed figurine.

"I never should have dragged you along to this thing. I thought you wouldn't be safe at home. Was I ever wrong."

"I had the situation fully under control. How was your meeting with the one they call Brent?"

"He never showed up. I waited by the back door, and nothing. Texted and tried calling. Musicians are so flaky. Get in."

I did as she instructed and slid down low in the passenger seat. Scarlet started the car. Her phone rang. She looked at the screen, then dropped it back into her bag.

"That's China. She can wait. She didn't feel like helping me tonight; I'm not going to listen to any of her drama."

We pulled out of the lot, onto the street that ran alongside the tracks. We drove for a few seconds, then Scarlet slowed down and pointed. The Phowl tour bus was parked on a dark side street.

"Look. Brent must be here. We probably just missed each other." She groaned. "I'm so sick of dealing with unreliable people. It's like I can never leave Maine or that world behind. Everybody is in their own heads, living on their own schedule. I can respect independence but people need to be there for each other, you know?"

"Totally."

"I'll pull over and see what he wants."

"No. Let me do it."

"Are you sure?"

"I'm sure. I need a quest to make me feel whole. Besides, you've done all the driving."

"What if he doesn't want to talk to you?"

"I'll tell him that I'm going to cast a Spell of Lameness on him, with a +2 Potion of Uncoolness."

Scarlet laughed. "That'll probably convince him. Sure you don't want me to come?"

"I have Prince Shieldhart with me. I fear nothing."

"That's what worries me."

She was still giggling as I hopped out of the car and over to the tour bus. The side door was slightly ajar; I knocked several times, loudly, then pried it open with my hands.

I went up into the front cabin. It was a total mess, and stank like nothing I'd ever smelled before. Stale smoke, incense, dirty socks, fast food, rancid booze and other nasty odors that I couldn't define. I felt my way carefully over the plastic bags, random newspapers and magazines, and little pieces of organic matter, and pushed my head through the curtain separating the cabin from the main section of the bus. I still couldn't see anything. Stupid Night Vision potion. I made a note to complain to Aku when I had the chance. I held Prince Shieldhart in front of me with one hand, and groped in the darkness with the other.

"Brent? You here? It's Scarlet's friend, Bert. Are you there?"

There was no answer. Then my toe hooked on something and I tripped. I put my hands down to break my fall and Prince Shieldhart flew out of my hand.

"Prince Shieldhart! No!"

I felt around me. My hand went into something wet. I pulled it back and sniffed. It smelled like ketchup. I tasted it. I was right.

A horn started honking, over and over. I backpedaled out of the van the way I'd come and stumbled down to the pavement. Scarlet was waving frantically from her car. I looked at her and she jabbed her finger toward the street, to my left. I looked over and saw a band of Orcs massing outside the K of C Hall. One of them saw me.

"There he is! He took Prince Shieldhart! Get the human scum!"

There was a tremendous roar and the gang of players came thundering towards me. Luckily most of them were not in the greatest physical condition, not to mention the clumsy armor, swords, and other gear most of them were carrying, but they were closing the gap between me and Scarlet quicker than I liked. I bolted for the car and got in.

"Did you see Brent?"

"No, but I lost Prince Shieldhart."

"Who?"

Something whizzed by the window. Scarlet screamed.

"What was that?"

"I'm not sure."

I looked in the side mirror. I saw one of the Orcs holding up a bow and drawing back. A projectile hit the back windshield and stayed there.

"What just hit us?"

"Looks like a suction tip," I said. "These guys aren't messing around. Let's get out of here."

Scarlet sped away just ahead of the mob, checking the rearview as she weaved through the dark streets. Then she started laughing so hard that it triggered a coughing fit. A couple of blocks later she pulled over to the curb.

"Can you...? I mean...were they serious? A bunch of nerds in Halloween costumes attacking us with Nerf arrows? I mean, can you imagine? Meanwhile, Brent is probably inside, looking for us. Hold on, this might be him."

Scarlet looked at her phone, sighed and answered.

"What's up, Chi? You what? Seriously? They are? Hold on, we'll be right over. Yes, I'm still with Bert. He's fine. No, Brent blew me off or we just missed each other. I'll pull in behind Elmo's. Okay, I'll be careful."

Scarlet clicked off the phone, checked to see that the way was clear, then pulled back onto the road.

"What's going on?"

"That was China. She said some of the bikers have been camped outside her building all night, and that they might have broken into her yoga studio. She can't get to her car; she's afraid to leave. We're going on a rescue mission."

"Cool," I said, feeling a new rush of warmth through my body from the Far Out, "Just show me where those bikers are and I'll hug the stuffing out of them."

"I'm half tempted to let you try," Scarlet drawled.

CHAPTER 12: CHINA CALLING

The yoga studio was in a lonely stretch of Main Street, where it flattens out for nearly a mile before winding down the steep hill past the library. As we approached, I kept alert for biker gangs and Orcs and giant panda bears, in that order.

"Won't they see us?"

"Not if they're all out front. Let's just hope they didn't think to have someone guarding the back. China said she didn't see anyone back there."

Scarlet turned off of Main Street and pulled in behind Elmo's Pizza. There was a municipal parking lot in the back that was nearly empty. We pulled around to the farthest aisle and found a spot against a high chain-link fence overgrown with vines. Scarlet grabbed her phone and tapped her thumbs.

"I'll text China that we're here."

There was a roar of engines. Scarlet said a bad word. I turned my head and watched the entrance. A big, slow-moving motorcycle rumbled into the lot. It was followed by a second bike. Then a third.

"Oh, no," Scarlet groaned. "I'd better tell China it's not safe." She texted frantically and hit send. "I just hope she hasn't left already."

One of the bikers turned on a powerful flashlight and moved it around the lot. The beam pierced inside the car and stayed there. The engines began revving again.

"What are we going to do?"

"Would they recognize your car?"

"I don't know. I doubt it. Luckily, I switched my plates from Maine to New York right after moving back. But they would definitely recognize me."

The bikes lurched forward and began zooming across the lot in our direction.

"Kiss me."

"What?"

"I saw it in a movie. Kiss me!"

I grabbed Scarlet by the back of the head and pulled her to me, and pressed my lips hard against hers. The touch of her lips made the Far Out explode once again in my system. Her hair became rivers of gold, running through my fingers. Scarlet made a few muffled mumbles, then a deep sigh seemed to escape her and she gave herself over to it. She slid a hand around my neck and grabbed my shoulder with the other hand. She smelled like sun and flowers and her lips felt like marshmallow kittens swimming in honey. The bikers pulled up behind the car and blasted the light directly on us. I started to pull back in a huff, ready to tell the bikers to cut it out, but Scarlet grabbed me harder.

I'd always said that Aria was the best kisser in the world—period, case closed—and even though she'd dumped me, I didn't feel the need to change my mind. But let's just say that Scarlet was no slouch in that department, either. I didn't know if it was natural ability, age, or experience, or a combination of all three, but she had a knack for locking lips that made kissing her exciting in different ways. I couldn't wait to tell people that I'd made out with a lesbian.

One of the bikers banged his hand on the back of Scarlet's car. We both jumped. I peeked over the seat. The biker grinned like an idiot and gave me a thumb's up. One of the other bikers barked at him and the three of them roared out of the parking lot.

"That was close," Scarlet gasped. "I've never been so scared in my life. My heart is pounding."

"My heart's pounding too but not only from fear," I said. Scarlet stroked my face.

"That's sweet. That was some really smart, quick thinking, Bert Shambles. You're not a half-bad kisser, either."

"For a guy."

She cocked an eye at me. "Riiight. Hold on, I think China texted me back." Scarlet consulted the phone. "Is she kidding? She says she needs us to come to her. She wants to get her video equipment out of the studio in case her place gets broken into again. What do you say? I'll tell her no way unless you think you'd be okay with that."

"I'm game," I said. "Let's help her."

"That's what I love about you, man. For a young guy you're such a righteous dude."

We got out of the car and walked along the fence until we came to an opening, a narrow alley that went behind the row of stores. I kept checking the entrance and listening for signs of the bikes. We followed the alley to a door with the sign HERGA STUDIO on it, and a bare bulb beaming down. Scarlet pressed the doorbell. Almost instantly, the door unlatched and swung open.

"Get in, quick."

We did as China told us and slipped into the small entryway. China slammed the door and locked and latched it.

"Let's get the equipment and get out of here. It's all in the back office," China said. "It's ready to go."

She unlocked a side door and we passed through another small passageway with two staircases, one leading up and the other down.

"Where do these go?" I asked.

"One goes to the basement, which I never go down into unless I have to. The other leads up to my apartment."

"What's in the basement?"

"Old boxes, equipment, inventory—from when the shop was here."

"What shop?"

"My dad had a hardware store back in the 80s, during one of his many failed periods of trying to lead a normal life. It didn't work very well. I could have, because my dad was really good with his hands and could fix anything. He bought the building for really cheap and fixed it up himself. I remember being so proud of him. Then he went to jail for a long time and I took over and put in a yoga studio."

"Where's your dad now?"

"I don't want to talk about it."

China opened the other door and then we were at the end of a long hallway with several more doors leading off the corridor. We went to the first door and China unlocked it. It was a small office. There were several bags on the floor, as well as a metal-reinforced case and a laptop bag.

"This is all of it. I've got my life savings invested in this equipment and I can't afford to lose any of it."

"Don't you have insurance?"

"Yeah, but not enough to cover everything. The premiums are killing me as it is."

"So where did they break in?"

"After the last time, I had new locks installed. This time they jimmied the back door. Luckily, it wasn't too badly damaged. I almost didn't realize it until I saw my stuff had been gone through."

"This time? You mean it's happened before?"

"Third time this year. It's crazy. I never had a problem for years and now it keeps happening. The cops think it's because of the economy. People are getting desperate so they take what they can get. Which isn't much in a yoga studio, except for this equipment."

"Then why didn't they take it?"

"I usually keep it up in my apartment. Either they don't know that I live upstairs or maybe they don't want to risk it. For all they know I could have a dog up there. I brought all the stuff down here to be ready for you guys. Think it will fit?"

"It's going to be tight. I'm more concerned that we won't be able to get out of here without the Wheels seeing us."

"Don't forget you drank a Potion of Invisibility earlier," I said. "Although my Night Vision didn't work very well in the van."

"What's he talking about?"

"Never mind. Let's get these bags to the car. We escaped the bikers once. I don't know if we can do it again."

We got the bags and cases. Scarlet and I carried two each, and China put the laptop bag over her shoulder and carried the last bag. She let us go first, and turned off the lights and locked the doors behind us. When we got to the exit, she checked the alley, then motioned with her head and we all went down the alley and cut right along the fence. Scarlet opened the hatchback.

"I have to put the back seats down."

Scarlet climbed in and lowered the back seats. We shoved the bags and cases in. It all fit, barely. Scarlet slammed the back and got into the driver's side. Then she got out again.

"What are you two waiting for?"

"There's only one seat," China said.

"Oh, for goodness sake, you'll have to sit on Bert's lap."

"Are you kidding me?"

"You're the one who had to bring all that equipment along when we're being chased by a bunch of psychos on motorcycles. Now get your butt in or you can just forget it!"

I'd never seen Scarlet angry before. She was mad, but she still did it in a nice way. China didn't say any more; she stood aside so I could get in. I slid into the seat and she squeezed on top of me. She was wearing tight black leggings and a skimpy shirt, which didn't leave much to the imagination.

"Tell Santa what you want for Christmas," I said.

China snickered against her will. "Shut up, you pervert."

"Both of you guys shut up. I've got to get us out of here and I can't see if you're both horsing around."

Scarlet maneuvered the car back like an expert, then turned us around and headed for the exit.

"Keep your eyes peeled for any of the bikers."

"They were hanging around my car," China said, "which is about a block up, to the left. So you should go right."

We rolled up to the exit and waited to turn onto Main. Elmo's Pizza was to the left. As Scarlet craned her neck forward to look for oncoming traffic, a large figure came out of the pizzeria, holding a slice. He glanced toward the car, then turned and stared.

It was Lizard.

"Oh, crap," Scarlet said.

"Go!" I screamed. "Go go go go!"

Scarlet floored it. The little car struggled under the heavy load it was carrying. We narrowly missed an oncoming car. The driver honked, screamed, and gave us a Long Island salute. If you don't know what that is, it involves raising a hand with only one finger extended. I'll leave the rest to your imagination.

CHAPTER 13" WE TOTALLY RAN AWAY

Scarlet made a series of evasive moves, turning left then right, left then right. I held on tight. My face was pressed into China's back, between her shoulder blades. I had a mouthful of her hair. She smelled good, very, with a delicate perfume mingled with a touch of sweat. I find the smell of sweat incredibly attractive on a woman. Then again, I'm 23 years old. There isn't much that I don't find attractive on a woman. I breathed her scent deeply and squeezed her.

"What the hell are you doing?"

"Sit on me, you fool."

"I am sitting on you, though I really wish I weren't. Scarlet, can you get this freak to stop?"

"Relax, Chi. Bert's just being your seatbelt."

"That's right," I purred, nestling into her hair. "Just think of me as a human seatbelt. A flesh seatbelt of love."

"I'm going to puke."

"Hold on, guys," Scarlet said. "I need you both to pay attention. We're almost there."

"Where are we going?"

"My place. But only if the coast is clear."

Scarlet turned off the headlights and rolled slowly onto her street. We went over the crest of the hill and started slowly down toward the cul-de-sac. Scarlet was coasting now, gently pumping the brakes to slow our descent.

"See anything?"

"Not yet."

"I can feel them," I said. "The bad men are near."

"Shh," China scolded. "This isn't a joke."

"I'm not joking. Behind the bushes on the left."

Scarlet hit the brakes. "You see them? Where?"

"Ignore him," China said. "There's nobody there."

Scarlet continued the roll. We saw them just in time. As the cul-de-sac opened to the circle, there were some overgrown hedges on our left. Tucked behind them I caught sight of the front forks and tires of several motorcycles.

I pointed. "There! Just like I told you! The Night Vision potion works!"

"That was impressive," China said. "How did you say you did that?"

"Shh," Scarlet whispered. "How am I supposed to get out of here without drawing attention to us?"

"Can you back up?"

"The hill's kind of steep. But I can try." She braked, put the car in reverse. "Let's hope for the best, people."

Scarlet started backwards up the hill. The engine whined and whinnied but we inched back up the hill slowly. We were almost to the top when China shifted her weight and my thigh muscle spasmed. I cried out in pain, more from the shock than pain.

"What is it?"

"My leg just got a cramp! Move a little to the right."

China shifted her weight. My knees swung out and knocked something. The engine revved loudly. We started rolling forward.

"You knocked it into neutral! Move your leg! China, squeeze to the right!"

"I'm trying," China cried. "But the hobo here is squirming."

"Ow ow ow!" I cried.

"Guys!"

We rolled all the way down and coasted straight into the center of the cul-de-sac. There were four bikers, resting on their seats, arms folded and eyes closed. One of them opened his eyes, still sleepy, and looked at us—first with an easy expression, then his eyes sharpened and his features got mean. He slapped one of the other guys awake.

Scarlet wiggled the shifter furiously. I grabbed China's rear with both hands and pulled her over. She grunted as her forehead hit the passenger window.

"Hit it!" I yelled, just as Scarlet found the gear. She floored the Toyota and spun it around the circle and raced back up the hill. The little motor didn't roar like the Olds, but the car performed well and we got to the crest of the hill just as the roar of the Harley engines started.

"Left! Left!"

Scarlet spun left. We were on a winding road through a quiet subdivision. It went down, banked right, then another quick left. We could keep going straight up another hill or make a right. Scarlet yanked the wheel right. We were in another dense tangle of winding streets. When we were halfway down that street, I saw the reflection of the motorcycle headlights in the side mirror, turning down after us.

"They saw us," I cried. "We have to keep moving."

"There's no way I can outrun them," Scarlet gasped. There was the tremble of fear in her voice.

"Maybe we don't have to," I said.

"What do you mean?"

"Make a right at the next corner, then look for a place to pull over."

"Pull over? They'll catch us for sure!"

"They're going to catch us anyway."

I remembered the neighborhood we were in from my elementary school days. I had a good friend who lived nearby. There was a small patch of woods that we sometimes cut through, one of those oddly-shaped remainder lots that hadn't been developed. I just hoped it was still there.

Scarlet made the turn. "Over there," I said. "Pull into those bushes."

"This is suicide," China groaned.

Scarlet pulled off to the side and underneath the overhanging bushes. She put the car into park and turned off the engine. We huddled together in the front bucket seats, our arms around each other the best we could manage.

"Been nice knowing you," Scarlet said.

Something came over me. It might have been the drugs but it felt like something much more powerful. My body filled with breath and I spoke in a voice I didn't recognize:

Spirit of shadow, spirit of night
Make us invisible to the sight
Of those who seek to cause us harm
Something something something charm!

The bikes turned the corner and roared onto the street. As they approached the car, the noise became unbearable. I couldn't look. Then the roaring went past the car and the sound got fainter, the burps and farts of the tailpipes echoed into the night until they were invisible—or whatever the word is that means invisible to the ears.

We pulled ourselves apart slowly.

"Wait—where did they go?"

"I don't believe it," China said. "They went right by us."

"Like we were *invisible*. Oh, my God, Bert, you did it! The spell worked!"

China scoffed. "Come on. You don't believe that, do you?"

"Of course! How would you explain it?"

"I'd say that you pulled over so perfectly that when they rounded the corner they didn't see you tucked into the bushes."

"There's no way they couldn't see us. What do you think, Bert?"

"I really need to pee," I said. "Let's get moving."

"Where?" China asked. "My place is out, obviously."

"So's mine," Scarlet added. "That leaves you, Captain Trips."

"Sure," I said. "My place is groovy."

"Thank you, Bert. We'd be delighted to be your guests."

I gave Scarlet directions for how to get to the rooming-house. The little dead-end street where I live is one of those places that very few people know about; even cab drivers usually have to be given directions.

We pulled up in front of the rundown, two-story tarpaper fire trap that I called home and got out of the car. China was horrified.

"You call this groovy? I've seen halfway houses that are nicer than this place."

"I think by law they have to be," I said.

"Come on, Chi, Bert is being really cool by letting us stay here. Let's get your bags upstairs."

We unpacked the car and lugged the bags up the walk to the front door. I was getting it open when Scarlet drew in her breath sharply and dropped the bags she was carrying.

"What's wrong?"

"It's my back. It goes out on me sometimes." Her eyes twinkled at me. "That's one of the things you have to look forward to when you get older," she said.

"Leave the bags, I'll come back down and get them."

"You sure? Okay, I won't argue. But I'll stay here and keep an eye on them until you get back."

I led China upstairs and into my room. She looked around and whistled.

"Man, you really need to learn how to practice some self-love. You ever think of actually cleaning this dump?"

"It is clean."

I went back down and got the other two bags. Scarlet followed me up.

"Oh, look how cute this place is!" She looked at the TV and the equipment. "Is this the stuff your girlfriend sent you?"

"Some of it. The rest is in the closet."

"Do you have a picture of her?"

I opened the dresser and pulled out the bikini shot. Scarlet whistled.

"Holy cow, she's gorgeous."

China looked over her shoulder, then back at me.

"You're actually going out with that dish? You're putting us on."

"I was, and I'm not."

"They just broke up," Scarlet explained.

"Why, did she finally see where you live?"

"If you don't like it you can sleep in the car," I said.

"I might have to. How are we supposed to fit on that tiny thing?"

We looked at my cot. It definitely looked small and sad. Scarlet walked carefully over to it, one hand on her back.

"Come on, Chi, we can do it. Remember at Bonnaroo? Three of us fit inside one sleeping bag."

"First of all, it was Burning Man, not Bonnaroo. Second, that was three slim women, not two women and a greasy, smelly man who's tripping his face off."

"Okay, then," Scarlet said firmly. "You can sleep in the car. And if those bikers come back you can just tell them not to bother you, because they're sweaty, greasy men too. Okay?"

China paused and turned around.

"On second thought, maybe I'll try the cot. But don't get any ideas, breeder boy."

"I think what she's referring to," Scarlet explained, "is that the third part of Far Out is a kind of imitation Viagra. The guy who invented Far Out wanted couples who took the drug to be able to cap off the night the right way."

I don't know how they did it. My cot is narrow, barely wide enough for me, but Scarlet and China worked themselves around me somehow, one on each side, nestled into the crook of each arm. China protested at first, saying my armpits smelled like Jerry Garcia's jockstrap after an Acid Test—I didn't know what she meant by that but I knew it wasn't a compliment—but by then even she was too tired to fight anymore and we got into a snug position, locked together like a human jigsaw puzzle. Combined with the effects of the Far Out it was like having two kittens dipped in melted butter purring on either side of me. They got into every nook and cranny; I was suspended in a sea of warm, sweet flesh. The street lamp outside threw a ray of light through the torn curtains and illuminated the scene. Even their scents took on a visible form: billowing purple clouds and pink hearts. Yellow moons and green clovers.

For once I felt like the world's biggest stud. Take that, Aria.

China stirred. She lifted her head.

"I told you no funny business, Shambles."

"I heard you the first time," I said.

"Really? Then why is the sheet levitating?"

I looked. "It's just being friendly," I said.

"Make it stop."

"Not possible."

"He's right," Scarlet said. "This is what I was talking about, where that imitation Viagra takes over. Just deal with it, Chi."

"How can I? It's gross."

"Do not fear my power. I come in peace."

"You come near me with that thing and it *will* be in pieces," she growled.

CHAPTER 14: 3 PEAS 1 POD

You could have put chalk outlines around us. Not that there was any room to move, with the three of us mashed together like that, but we fit together so perfectly that it felt like we'd clicked into some kind of human jigsaw puzzle that formed a picture of a snuggle-sleep machine. I woke up before dawn with my arms still around the two women. If I could have reached my phone, I'd have snapped a picture.

I lay for what seemed like a long time, taking in their scents, listening to the peaceful, shallow breathing. Then I dozed off. When I opened my eyes again the sun was up. My arms were numb from being under the girls all night. My head swam and felt fuzzy, like it was filled with cotton balls. I turned my head to the left and saw Scarlet peeking up at me from my armpit, smiling. I blinked at her. Then China stirred. She pushed a few strands of hair out of her face and managed a slight smile.

"Good morning," Scarlet sing-songed. "How did you two angels sleep?"

"Great," I said. "How about you, China?"

"Surprisingly well, actually." She made a motion as if to climb over me and out of the cot, then stopped.

"Really? Can't you please do something about that?"

Scarlet and I looked. The circus was still in town.

"That's strange," Scarlet said. "The effects of the Viagra substitute should have worn off by now."

"It's not the Viagra," I said. "I wake up like this every morning."

"That is way too much information," China said.

"I'm a normal, healthy young man. It happens when the wind blows. But I can roll on my side if it'll make it easier for you." I rolled onto my left side, facing Scarlet.

"Is that a circus tent or are you just happy to see me?" she said, in her best Mae West impression. We both giggled at this as China smoothly hopped out of the cot.

"What's the plan?"

"I can't stay here, that's for sure. We have classes starting in less than an hour, so I really have to get downtown and open the studio. Can you drive me? I need to take a shower."

"I'll take you, but I can't be rushed. Not after what I went through last night. I'm sure Bert will let you use his shower if you ask nicely enough."

"I want to get clean, not dirtier," she said.

"Then you'll just have to walk to the studio," Scarlet said.

China huffed. "Fine. Bert, may I please use your shower?"

"Of course. I have brand new towels in the closet. There's a robe in there too, that's never been used. It has a big 'A' on it."

"You have his and hers bathrobes?" Scarlet asked. "Were they from Aria?"

"Who else?"

"That's sweet. And kind of sad too, of course."

China got the towels and bathrobe from the closet, as well as my toiletry kit with the soap and shampoo. She accepted it all with something approaching gratitude.

"Thanks," she said. "So where's the bathroom?"

"Across the hall. Oh, and if you see a guy in a purple robe and wizard's hat, don't be frightened. He's harmless."

China looked at me strangely with this last comment, then went out to do her business. Scarlet stayed where she was, pressed against me.

"Do you have anything planned for today?" I asked. She shook her head.

"Nope. I'm free, today and every day. I could sleep until noon. What time is it?"

I craned my neck to see the clock. "7:30."

"Mmmm," she crooned, burying closer to me. "Only four and a half hours to go."

"Don't you have to drive China to the studio?"

"Mmmm, don't remind me. You really know how to spoil a girl's mood." She opened her eyes and sighed. "Okay, boyfriend. You win. Time I got this creaky old body up and did some stretches."

Scarlet got out of the cot and sat on the floor, in the one small area that was not taken up by China's camera equipment or my mess.

"I definitely did something to my back last night," she said, rubbing a spot above her right butt cheek. "I should be fine after I do my morning routine."

"Here?"

"Sure. It's a little tight, but I can manage."

I lay on my side and watched as Scarlet pretzeled her body into one unnatural position after another. I had a primo view. I loved how un-self-conscious she was. She had stripped out of her T-shirt and cut-offs and was wearing nothing but a little tank top and skimpy French-cut panties. I was pleased to note that, unlike my previous ideas about hippies being hairy, Scarlet was smooth everywhere that I could see.

Scarlet lay on her belly then pushed the front of her torso up.

"No offense, but for someone who's in such great shape that's a pretty lame pushup."

"It's not a pushup, it's the cobra pose." She finished that and got into a standing position. "Now for the downward-facing dog."

In one fluid motion she pulled herself back so she was sitting on her heels, hands stretched out in front of her. Then she pushed up onto her feet and hands, in an upside-down V-shape. It gave me a perfect view of the back of her panties.

Then I heard the noise.

"Oh!" Scarlet cried. "Ow ow ow ow."

"What is it?"

"That was my back. Hoo boy, this is bad." She grimaced and winced.

"What is it? What's wrong?"

"I can't straighten up. My back has locked up completely. I need help." She was in intense pain, on the verge of tears.

I got out of bed and stood next to her. "What do I do?"

"Try lifting me up. Very slowly."

I got around in front of Scarlet and took hold of her upper arms.

"Now gently lift."

I did as she asked. It was going well until Scarlet's head came into contact with the front of my boxer briefs.

"My God," she gasped, "doesn't that thing ever take a break?"

This made us both laugh, which made the situation worse.

"Ow! Stop! Put me back down!"

I lowered her back into the dog position.

"Try lifting me from behind. Maybe if you support my waist, I can do the rest."

I did as she asked and got behind her. I leaned over and hugged her midsection, my cheek almost resting on her back.

"Just be careful of that weapon you go there, cowboy."

"Maybe I should get China out of the shower."

"There's no time. My arms can't hold like this much longer. The pain is bad. Please!"

"Okay. On the count of three. One...two...three!" I pulled. Scarlet howled in pain.

"What should I do? Should I stop?"

"No! Don't stop! Just keep that thing out of my butt!"

"I'm trying! Don't make me laugh!"

"Just pull me harder! And don't stop this time!"

I stepped back. "Hold on, maybe I can adjust this thing." The girls were right; it really was ridiculous down there.

"No!" Scarlet cried. "Don't let go of me! Your penis is fine where it is! Get back here!"

"I'm coming, I'm coming!"

I went back to her. I had her good now. I grunted and pulled but still needed more leverage.

"Forgive me, Scarlet, I'm not getting fresh but I have to reach close to your breasts."

"Go ahead! Grab my tits! Just don't stop this time!"

I cupped my hands over her breasts, pressed the tent pole into the lace panties for extra leverage and gave a final yank upward. With a long, final cry of pain Scarlet straightened halfway. She was almost upright.

"We're doing it! Just a few more inches! Don't stop!"

There was a clacking sound, then a creaking. The door to my room swung open. I looked up. A small figure stood in the hallway, next to a suitcase.

It was Aria.

She was tan and in a smart outfit, roller bag behind her. Our eyes met and the big smile on her face dropped as she took in the scene, of me standing in my underwear with my hands cupped around the boobies of a nearly naked blonde. Scarlet's head was still hanging down.

"Wow. That was intense. I don't know if I'll be able to walk after that." She pushed the hair out of her eyes. "Oh, hi!" she said brightly. "You must be Aria! Oh my gosh, we were just talking about you!"

I was about to make the introductions when the bathroom door opened across the hall. China came out, wrapped in the bathrobe with the big 'A' on it, pulling a comb through her wet hair. She looked at Aria.

"Aren't you Bert's ex-girlfriend? What are you doing here?"

Aria's mouth dropped. She didn't say anything. She appeared to be in a state of deep shock. Then her face registered a spasm of intense pain, a look of wounded confusion that I'd never forget.

"It's not what you think!" I cried.

I came out from behind Scarlet, arms outstretched. Aria took one look at the front of my boxer briefs and screamed, then dropped the handle of her wheelie bag and ran down the stairs. China watched her go, then snorted.

"I can see why you two broke up. She's really uptight."

CHAPTER 15: NOW YOU TELL ME

By the time I got my clothes on and made it downstairs, Aria was no longer in sight. I pulled the wheelie bag behind me, down Cheshire Lane. It was slow going with the bag. The road is pretty rough, and steep, so it kept tipping over, and I still couldn't use my left arm very well. I made it to the bottom of the hill and took a left, toward Route 59. When I got there I looked both ways. She was heading south, toward the train station. She already had a good lead. I called her name a few times but she ignored me. She finally got held up at an intersection and I came up alongside her, out of breath. She yanked her arm away before I could touch her.

"Stay the hell away from me! I swear, if you so much as touch me I'll kill you!"

The exertion must have re-triggered some of the Far Out still in my system, because I got a huge, goofy grin that I couldn't control.

"You think this is funny? I'll show you funny!"

She swung directly into my left forearm. It was like being shot all over again. I dropped the wheelie bag and grabbed it. "That really hurts," I said, fighting back tears. "That's my bad arm."

"Good. Maybe one of your bimbos can rub it and make it feel better."

"They do yoga, not massage."

"You want another one?"

"No!"

"'*Oh, Aria, I forgot my appointment, because I was hanging with my blonde yoga-girl-person.*' Funny, I don't see a cast on your arm. I can't even conceive of what would make you tell such a twisted lie. Were you trying to torture me, make me feel sorry for you while you cheated on me?"

"I can explain about the cast, and I wasn't fooling around with them!"

"You're right. You were only with one of them. The other one had already gone in to take a shower, wearing *my* robe, the robe *I* sent you, with *my* initial on it. What kind of person would do that?"

"I'm sure she doesn't care about what initial was on it," I said. Aria screamed and raised her hand again. I dodged it this time.

"Chill! Can we talk?"

"There's no point. Let me ask you, is your little blonde hottie moving in?"

"No, why would you say that?"

"I saw all that luggage on your floor. Taking a trip together?"

"No! God, you're so paranoid. That was video equipment."

Now, I've been told sometimes that I 'think out loud,' meaning I speak before I think things through. This was one of those times. Aria turned crazy red. I seriously thought the top of her head was going to explode. A big vein throbbed on her forehead, her teeth clenched and she shook all over with rage. She got so crazy that she started yelling in Italian, and based on the way she emphasized certain words I'm glad I didn't understand. The only words I recognized were *idiota* and *puttana*. That was enough.

The light changed. Aria kept moving. We had made it to the train station, and now started across the parking lot, me still wheeling her bag. When we got to the station house I was so out of breath I thought I was having a heart attack. I threw the bag down so it made a big noise.

"Enough! Stop!"

I sat on a bench, sweat pouring out of me.

"You have to believe me, nothing happened."

"Really? Then you're telling me you didn't have your hands on that half-naked *puttana's* breasts? You're telling me you weren't standing there in your underwear, with your...*thing* sticking out? How stupid do you think I am? You're such a typical man. My brothers are exactly the same. *'I was just holding the gun. I didn't shoot the guy...I don't know how that suitcase full of money and drugs got into the trunk of my car...What hooker?'* Always innocent. You're just as bad as they are."

"First of all, those women are lesbians."

"I'm sure all the men who watch your sick videos will appreciate that."

"It wasn't sex! It was yoga!"

"Is that what you call it?" Aria looked at her fingernails and spoke in a low voice.

"I don't know why you're trying to lie your way out of this, but it's not going to work. I heard everything from outside your door. *'Oh, stick it in my butt, ooh ahhh ooh ahhh...faster, harder, I'm coming...'.* It was disgusting."

"For your information, she was telling me *not* to stick it in her butt."

"And that other one. Wearing the robe that *I* bought! Why did she have to wear my robe?"

"Because my robe would have been too big!"

It had been weeks since Aria had last slapped me, mainly because she was three thousand miles away. Now I got my second one in just a few minutes. I didn't remember it hurting as much before. I think all that rest and relaxation and healthy living she had gotten out in California had made her stronger. She moved to hit me again but I grabbed her wrist.

"Don't hit me again, ever, without my permission. Do you understand?"

"Ow! Yes, I understand."

I dropped her wrist and she rubbed it.

"Can I slap you?" she asked.

"Can you do it gently?"

"Probably not."

"Then no."

She plopped down on the platform and started crying.

"What are you even doing here?" I asked. "Did you bring your new man to introduce me to him?"

"What are you talking about?"

"Now who's lying? You told me yourself, over the phone. You were on his boat and had to go."

"Is that what you think?" Aria threw her head back, eyes closed, and let out a long, low groan. "That explains all those crazy texts you sent."

"Don't change the subject. You go away for the weekend on your new boyfriend's yacht and that's fine, but all I do is have a couple of women sleep over at my place and suddenly I'm the bad guy. What texts?"

"Later that night, after we got cut off. I didn't get them until we pulled into port. Don't you remember?"

"I was drunk."

"That's another thing. You drink too much. Have you ever considered that there might be a connection?"

"Between drinking and getting drunk? I was aware of the connection, yes."

"Never mind. You're not going to understand."

"I understand, I just won't let you weasel out of it so easily. This started with your phone call, don't try to blame my drinking."

"Sure. Even if your drinking ends with you *not* poking your lesbian girlfriends in the butt?"

"I'll have you know that I wasn't drunk last night. I was on drugs."

"Delightful. I feel so much better now."

She pulled out her phone.

"Since you don't believe me you can read them for yourself."

She turned the phone around and showed me the screen.

Hav fun w yr new dood
Im hangn wif my hawt nu gf
Blnd bmbshll
We do 'yoga' haha
p.s. ur fat

And then, at 3:28 a.m.:
Do u need a watr filtr?

I waved the phone away.

"I get it," I said. "What do you want me to say? That I was jealous of you for being on a boat with your new boyfriend while I sweated it out here trying to earn a living? That I was upset being stuck alone here fending for myself while you were sunning yourself on the beach? That I felt insulted that you thought sending me piles of stuff was supposed to make me miss you less, or feel less lonely? Is that what you want me to say?"

As the words came out of my mouth, instead of just spinning around my head, I realized for the first time how angry I was about it, and how much it hurt. I was even more surprised to discover I was crying. Dr. K charges me twenty-five dollars per session. I think he's worth every penny.

Aria was different now too. When she spoke her voice was gentle and calm.

"I'm sorry. I didn't know that I was hurting you. I never meant to. You knew why I couldn't be here with you, at least for the summer, and I thought you knew how much it broke my heart. I sent you gifts because it was the only thing I could think of; it made me sad thinking you were stuck here with a cast on your arm. I only got you stuff I thought you'd like."

"I do, but it's too much. And all that stuff doesn't cure my loneliness, it only makes it worse. So I went to a stupid music festival at a park because an old woman invited me."

"Stop calling her old! I saw her; she looks our age. She's incredible."

"Okay, you're right. She's smoking hot."

"Totally."

"You can't believe how firm her breasts still are."

"Shut up."

"Whatever. The point is, it was totally innocent. It was the first and only invitation I've gotten since my trial ended, except for the crazy people who want to take me on UFO rides, or mobility-challenged shut-ins who want to plan a wheelchair wedding with me."

"Have you made any effort to do anything fun? Or do you just wait around for people to invite you places?"

"What does it matter? I was trying to have fun, isn't that something at least? It's not easy for me, no, since I've never been able to afford to do much of anything. I finally do something fun and a guy dies. Then I get home and find out the cable guy has been there and invaded my space, and then you're all like 'did you get the cable or not?'"

"What's your point?"

"Did I ever ask for cable?"

"Uh, yeah."

"I did?"

"All the time. You must have complained to me like a hundred times. That's mainly why I did it, just to shut you up. Wait a second, did you say someone died?"

"Whatever. It doesn't matter now. The point is, I can't escape from my problems like you, I have to face them every day. There's no San Diego for guys like me unless we join the Navy. And for your information, yes, the singer of the band died right in front of me, and then last night I almost OD'd on an experimental drug because I thought it was aspirin, and took a mini-figure that didn't belong to me, and then a bunch of nerds dressed like Orcs attacked us. To top it all off, there's some kind of crazy biker gang in town that started chasing us." I put my head in my hands. "I think I need to throw up."

"And just think, you said you never have any fun."

Aria got up and sat on the bench next to me. She put her arms around me and squeezed. She ran her fingers through my hair, rubbed my back, whispered sweet words while planting little kisses on my shoulders, my head, anywhere she could reach.

"It sounds like you've been through a horrible time. I hope you can forgive me. I want you to tell me all about it."

I pulled away from her. "Why? So you can have a good laugh with your rich new boyfriend?"

"What is this thing about a new boyfriend?"

"The last thing you said to me was 'I met someone' before you hung up."

"I didn't hang up! We were cut off because I was getting out of range of a signal. He's not a boyfriend, there's nothing romantic at all about it. He's like in his fifties and totally gross. And I was with my cousins; they're close friends with him and his wife. Didn't you get my other texts and calls?"

"I didn't read or listen to any of them."

"Gee, thanks. If you had, then you'd have understood, and I wouldn't have had to pack like a crazy woman and take the next red-eye flight so I could see you in person."

"Okay, you're here. What's the big deal?"

"You really want me to tell you?"

"Yes."

"The man I met. Captain Mickey. He might know where your dad is."

It wasn't what I was expecting. It hit me so hard that I sat up straight.

"You came all the way out here just to tell me that?"

"No. I came out here to get my boyfriend back."

That's when she planted the first kiss on me.

All the weeks and miles we'd been apart, all the bad feelings we'd built up, dissolved the moment our lips touched. Aria had returned, but I felt like the one who'd come home.

After a few perfect minutes swapping spit we finally pulled apart.

"So you understand now? It wasn't romantic, except toward you. I was hoping I could help you find your dad."

"All right, I understand. But who says I even want to find that bum at this point?"

"Don't you? I'd think it would be incredibly important to you. Don't you want to know if he's alive, or why he left, any of it?"

"I don't know. What did this Captain Mickey guy say?"

"He said he saw your dad at a place in St. John, in the Caribbean, about five years ago. They talked for a bit, but Mickey said your dad seemed really uncomfortable and left soon after."

"How were you even talking about him? How did the subject come up?"

"My cousins introduced me to him, and he said he lived in Mumfrey until about ten years ago, when he moved to San Diego. I mentioned that my boyfriend—that's you, by the way—that my boyfriend's dad used to be a sailor at the yacht club and he said he knew your dad. Jim Shambles."

Just hearing his name made me tense up.

"Did he say anything about why he left?"

"Yes. He said there were a lot of rumors going around the yacht club at the time, in the early 90s. A lot of people were saying that there was infidelity involved. But Mickey said he'd heard something else as well, that your dad had gotten involved in something very dangerous, and had to leave and change his identity in order to protect himself."

"I can believe the first one," I said. "My dad was a handsome guy, and knew lots of people. He gave sailing lessons. I'm sure every rich divorcee in town tried seducing him at least once. It still doesn't excuse him for ignoring me for all those years."

"You don't understand. Mickey didn't say it was your dad who cheated. He said it was your mom."

At that moment, a small part of my brain began to itch and burn. A small, nagging doubt deep in the back of my mind woke up. There had always been something about my mom's memory of that time that seemed overly vague to me, something about her hangdog manner, her habit of drinking too much, too regularly. Is that what she was hiding? Some kind of dumb suburban infidelity that went on about ten million times a day in this Christian country of ours?

I snapped out of it. "I don't care if she slept with the whole town. I didn't do anything to deserve it. He has no excuse."

"Maybe he—"

"Maybe he what? Isn't my father? Is that what you were going to say?"

"Forget it," she said quietly. "I'm sorry I brought it up."

"Sorry? Why? Because you flew three thousand miles just so you could call my mom a whore? And call me a bastard? So you could get your ignorant little revenge against me by making me feel even more like a loser? So you could feel even more superior to me?" I was screaming now. My neck burned with rage.

"That's not what I meant!"

"Of course not. It never is with your kind, you rich daughters of privilege and your charmed lives. Your definition of tragedy is when you don't get everything you want the second that you want it. The only pain you'll ever feel is when you occasionally have to do things for yourself."

"That's not true! I'm overtired; I'm not thinking clearly. Let's talk about this later."

"No. There's no point. You make me sick. I don't ever want to see you again. Don't worry, I'll return all your stuff. I know that's all you really care about, anyway."

I stood up to go. Aria sobbed until she gulped air. I started for home. I didn't look back. I don't know what it is. I've got this wiring in me that makes me freak out when I hear or see a woman being hurt. That includes my mom.

CHAPTER 16: A VISIT FROM THE LAW

It was a hazy morning, warm and muggy. My blood burned, my heart ached.

I jaywalked across Route 59 in front of oncoming cars. One driver had to hit the brakes hard. He leaned on the horn. I turned and bared my teeth and went toward him. I must have looked crazy because he sped on his way. I finished crossing and went into the 7-11 for coffee and an atomic bomb. They were out of atomic bombs so I made a coffee, took a bottle of water—the good stuff, from the refrigerator, even though it cost more—and a glazed donut. I didn't use the tongs for the donut, just put it into the wax bag with my fingers.

At the checkout counter the cover of the *Post* caught my eye:

PHOWL PLAY

Investigators looking into the death of hippie rocker Gavin Burns have said that the deadly shock that killed the singer-songwriter was caused by a faulty ground wire in the musician's amplifier.

The story was continued on an inside page. I paid for the stuff, went outside and sat on the bench in front of the store to continue reading.

A statement from the band's management said that the other band members and road crew are cooperating fully with the investigation. It said that the band had performed a sound check earlier in the day and there was no sign of anything wrong. "We're eager to have this matter resolved so that our beloved brother can rest in peace, and will do everything we can to bring the person responsible to justice," the statement concluded.

I finished my coffee, got up and walked back to my room. When I closed the door I could hear the muffled sound of my cellphone ringing. I remembered it was in the top drawer, where I'd left it. I got it out in time and answered. It was Scarlet.

"I'm so glad you answered. I just got home from dropping China and all her stuff at the studio. Someone broke into my house last night."

"Are you sure?"

"Definitely. The place has been gone through. It's not trashed, but it's messy. And I found a window propped open in one of the bedrooms upstairs."

"Where are you now?"

"In the kitchen. But I'm scared."

"Don't stay in the house. I'll be right over."

"How? Your car is here, remember?"

I had forgotten about that. "I'll take a taxi."

"Do you want me to come get you?"

"No. I need to take a shower first anyway."

"I'll be here. By the way, how did it go with Aria?"

"Don't ask."

"Aw, I'm sorry. Maybe it will still work out."

"I doubt it."

"Have a little faith, hometown hero. Take your time. I'm okay, really."

I took a long shower. I was no longer mad, just numb. I couldn't hate Aria, as much as I wanted to. She was spoiled and a bit clueless, but she had a no-nonsense, businesslike way about her that I found refreshing compared to other women I'd met. She was fierce and probably a bit crazy, but if so then she was also crazy enough to fly across country just to tell me she wanted to be my girlfriend. That was pretty amazing. And I knew she didn't really mean to hurt me or insult my mom, she was just passing along what she'd been told. But I didn't have time to worry about her feelings right then, either. I finished the shower, brushed my teeth, then went back across the hall, dried off and got dressed. I took my keys and wallet and started out.

"Going somewhere, Shambles?"

The voice startled me. I looked to my right and saw a shadowy figure coming up the stairs. It was my probation officer, Paul D'Addario. Or as I prefer to call him, Daddy-O.

"I'm on my way to meet a friend."

"You mean you were. You're not going anywhere just yet. Let's go into your room."

Somehow it all hit me at that moment, seeing him: Gavin, the horrible Martin guy trying to run me over, the drugs, the K of C hall, Martin again, Prince Shieldhart, the Nerf arrows, the biker gang, the chase, then Aria. I could be arrested for half the things I did the night before, and if Daddy-O found out about any of it or suspected I was up to no good I was screwed.

Daddy-O is a nice guy, but he also started dating my ex-girlfriend, the one who almost got me thrown in jail in the first place, as soon as the trial was over. So I didn't really respect his ethics very much, and couldn't be sure she wouldn't poison his mind against me in some way in the future. Not that I needed any help digging my own grave. I had a natural gift for getting myself into trouble.

I tried unlocking the door but I was shaking so much that I couldn't get the key into the lock without using both hands, and even then it was a struggle. So much for being a cool cucumber. I realized if I hadn't taken the shower I'd have gotten away before he arrived. Sometimes I really hated personal hygiene.

"You okay, Shambles? You were expecting me, weren't you?"

"Not for another week."

"I left you a message last night, saying I'd be coming by. Didn't you get it?"

"I was busy. I didn't check messages yet."

I got the door open and we went in. I sat on the edge of the cot. Daddy-O took the desk chair.

"So where were you last night?"

"When? I went a few places."

"Who were you with?"

"A couple of friends."

"Friends? That's good. You weren't at the Knights of Columbus hall by any chance, were you?"

"Why would you think that?"

"No reason. I understand there was quite a scene there last night. You didn't hear about it? What's the matter? You look pale."

I didn't know why he was playing cat and mouse, but it drove me crazy.

"Look, I can explain what happened, but you have to be patient. There was a lot going on and I don't want to forget anything that might be important later."

"Go on."

I tried saying something but only a squeak came out. My throat was so dry from nerves that I couldn't talk. I pointed to my throat, then the little dorm fridge against the opposite wall. I went to the fridge and took out a bottle of seltzer. I offered it to Daddy-O, but he waved me off. I took a deep sip and felt better.

"Okay," I said, "it was like this..."

Something on the desk caught Daddy-O's eye. There was a sheet of paper in the typewriter. He reached over, read what was on it, and yanked the page out.

"Is this what you're trying to tell me? It's not often we get such good clues in my business, let alone a signed confession."

I fell off the edge of the cot onto the hard wooden floor.

"Take it easy, Shambles. You're really on edge. Can't you tell when you're being messed with?" Daddy-O handed me the paper.

Dear Hometown Hero,

Last night was unforgettable. Hope we didn't break your poor little bed. You definitely fixed my back problem. My boobs feel better too :)

Sorry your gf didn't stick around longer. Hope she understands we had no choice but to sleep with you. Later gator.

Love, S and C

p.s. Chi sez thanx 4 the shower and robe. She'll let you know how the videos come out.

I could have kissed the letter. I handed it back to Daddy-O.

"You got me," I said sheepishly. "It's all true."

"So I take it you had quite a time last night?"

"You could say that."

"S and C, these are friends of yours? Lady friends, I presume?"

"Correct."

"This is what you were afraid to tell me? Why you've been so nervous?"

"You could say that."

"Did you really think you'd get in trouble for having fun with a couple of women?" He gave me a look. "They're not underage, are they?"

"No. They're both older than me, in fact."

He looked at the page again. "I like the 'Hometown Hero' bit," he chuckled. "Are you really getting that much action from what happened over the summer?"

"No, most of the people I meet are wackos. These two are the exception."

"Impressive. Believe it or not, I'm happy for you."

"You are?"

"Sure. It beats just sitting here, stewing about the past and feeling sorry for yourself. And now at least I know what you were doing when I was trying to call you last night."

I knew I was lying to Daddy-O by not telling him the whole story, but if he hadn't connected me to the events at the K of C hall, then I wasn't going to help him out, either. He wasn't a detective, he was a probation officer. I told myself it wasn't in his jurisdiction and felt better. I felt such an incredible sense of relief, in fact, that I got to my feet. I wanted to dance.

"Where do you think you're going?"

"Aren't we done?"

"Not quite. I haven't even told you why I'm here."

He reached into the pocket of his sport coat and pulled something out. It was a plastic container.

"What's that?"

"Specimen cup. I need a urine sample."

CHAPTER 17: AN ARREST IS MADE

I stood there, not moving, not sure I heard correctly.
"A what?"
"Sample. Of your urine. Pee test."
"Why?"
"It's part of your probation. It's random. I don't like it either." Daddy-O narrowed his eyes. "Why, are you worried that something might show up?"
"Me, worried? About what?" Except maybe the fact that I was tripping my face off the night before on an overdose of an experimental hallucinogenic? I wondered if the test could detect a designer drug like Far Out; I tried thinking of a way I could ask Daddy-O without arousing more suspicion. I couldn't.
He shook the cup at me.
"If you don't mind. I don't have all day."
I took the plastic vial. "I'll be right back. Or do I have to fill it here, in front of you?"
"That won't be necessary."
I went across the hall and into the bathroom. My head and heart were pounding. I opened the vial and put it on the sink counter. I filled the vial, then put it back on the counter so I could finish my business. Then I flushed and went to the sink to wash my hands. I heard a scream. That's when I realized that someone was in the shower. I had been so preoccupied with fear that I hadn't noticed.
Aku's head appeared from behind the shower curtain. He was wearing a shower cap. He didn't look pleased.

"I'm sure you're aware that flushing causes the shower to become scalding hot. Couldn't you please wait to use the bathroom? I'll be out in just a minute.

"I'm sorry," I mumbled. "I wasn't paying attention."

I went back into my room. Daddy-O was on a call.

"I don't care where we go for the weekend...it doesn't have to be Jersey...what? Why not?"

I knew he was talking to Devil Girl. I recognized the tension in his voice, the hollowing out of his manhood, and the unforgettable flushing sound of the toilet of despair that surrounded him. I'd been there too.

"I'm not being mean...what? Why? I can't...you know it's not...huh?"

He pulled the phone away from his ear and looked at it, in the universal reaction people have when someone hangs up on them. I smiled. He was learning what being with Devil Girl was really like. Sure, she was sexy and wild, exciting and unpredictable, but like any drug, once you got hooked on her your life went downhill fast, until it was pure hell. He was rapidly entering the downhill phase. Daddy-O turned to me.

"I can't believe how someone—" He saw my expression and stopped mid-sentence. "Never mind. Where's the cup?"

"I left it in the bathroom."

"We don't do the test here. I send it out to the lab."

"I'll get it."

I went across the hall. Aku had finished his shower; the bathroom was empty. The vial was on the counter. I took it and brought it back to Daddy-O, who had me place it into a plastic baggie. Then he peeled off a sticker and sealed the baggie with it.

"I'd better get going. I see you got a few new things." He motioned to the TV. "I'm glad to see you're treating yourself." He smiled. "Or is that what you and the girls watch your videos on? Never mind. I don't want to know."

Daddy-O left. I watched through the curtains as he got into his car, turned around and headed back down the street. I had dodged one problem, only to find myself with a much bigger problem. Story of my life. The irony was that I never did drugs, never liked them the few times I had experimented with them, and had only taken the Far Out by accident. Not that he was going to believe that.

I got myself together and went down to the train station and got a cab to Scarlet's. She was sitting on the front lawn, reading a book. It had been more than an hour since she'd called.

"I was beginning to worry that something had happened to you."

"I got delayed. Are you all right?"

"I'm fine. Just a little freaked out."

Not much had changed inside that I could see, except for a small closet in the entry way that had been gone through. Coats, umbrellas, and a few small boxes that had been pulled out and were on the floor.

"It's got to be Martin," I said.

"I don't think so."

"The guy is obsessed. He could have come by after the bikers left, seen that no one was home, and broken in."

"I'm pretty sure it wasn't him. Come upstairs and I'll show you why."

Scarlet led me upstairs. The first door on the left was a small home office. It was filled with boxes, piles of papers. The closet had been gone through, like the downstairs closet. Papers and overturned boxes were spilling out of it. Against the far wall there was a desk, with an open window above.

"This is where he came in. I haven't moved or changed anything. Watch out for pieces of glass."

We made our way through the maze of junk to the opposite wall. One of the panes of glass had been broken, to unlatch the window. There was part of a muddy footprint on the desk, but it looked too smudged to be of any use.

"This is where he came in. Whoever it was had to climb up onto the little roof over the den, then squeeze into the window. That's why I don't think it was Martin."

"How did he get onto the roof?"

"I don't know. Maybe a ladder?"

I looked out the open window onto the small roof area below where the intruder had entered.

"See anything?"

"Not from this angle. But we should go outside and check."

There were some overgrown bushes along the side of the den. A few of the smaller branches were bent back, and a few were snapped off. I found the broken pieces on the ground; they were still fresh and green. Then I crouched down and crawled partly under the shrubs; I saw two indents in the soil, about an inch down, spaced about eighteen inches apart. I pulled myself out and stood up, brushed the grass from my jeans.

"I'm no expert but it definitely looks like someone was here recently. Do you have a ladder?"

"I think so. It was usually hanging on the side of the garage if I remember."

We went to the side of the detached two-car garage in the rear of the property. There was an old wooden ladder hanging from some rusted hooks on the side. I checked the ladder and found some caked dirt on one end.

"It looks like the person used this."

"It certainly made things easy," Scarlet said. "I bet it was the Wheels. They were hanging outside here last night, and they were harassing China too. Which is crazy, since she never lived in Maine, never had any dealings with them."

"But then, why go through all the effort of chasing us? Sort of like with Gavin's death, doesn't it seem likely that we'd suspect them first?"

"They're a biker gang. They're a rough bunch, but it's not like they're criminal masterminds."

"Maybe they came back after we lost them and wanted to send a message, mess with your head."

"But it still looks like they were looking for something. Otherwise why go through the closets like that?"

"Can you think of any reason why they might be looking for something?"

Scarlet looked away. "Not really."

"Could it have something to do with what Lizard said to you at the concert, about you having something of theirs?"

"I don't know," she said quietly. "Maybe."

"Isn't it time you started trusting me? I mean, you hired me to go through your dad's stuff, even though you didn't know me at all."

"That's different. You were on TV."

"Very funny."

"I'm serious. It might sound crazy but I do trust you. A lot. Maybe more than I should. I'm a very trusting person by nature. I've been afraid that if you know, you'd lose respect for me. And believe it or not, I feel like I need your respect. It's important to me."

"That sounds like a line if I ever heard one."

"Fine. Have it your way. You want to know what they want?"

"Yes."

She put her hand on my stomach. "It's here."

"They want my rock-hard abs?"

"No, what's *in* your belly. That Far Out you took. They claim I stole it from them."

"Did you?"

"No! I took it from the guy who made it. Turns out he owed the Wheels some money and had promised them the Far Out as payment. Which is bull, because he owed me a lot more money than he owed them—he owed everybody in the scene up there. I was so mad at him by the time I left, and so upset about my dad, who was dying, that I found his stash of pills and took them."

"There weren't more than ten or twenty pills in that clay pot. How much are they worth?"

"They go for twenty bucks a pill."

"But that's still only a few hundred dollars."

"But that's only what's left. There were hundreds of pills originally. Maybe over a thousand."

"You stole twenty thousand dollars' worth of drugs?"

"It does sound like a lot, now that you mention it. That's why I can't call the police about any of this. I'm afraid the truth will come out, and I'll be in all kinds of trouble."

"What did you do with the pills?"

"Flushed them, of course! Except for the ones in the jar that you found. I wanted to keep some around in case they were ever needed for evidence, or to be analyzed. I even toyed with the idea of taking them, especially after my dad died, but I'm not really into escapism on that level. I'd rather meditate, or take a long hike in the woods. Drugs seem like a cheap shortcut to me."

"Me too. That's why I prefer alcohol."

Scarlet laughed. "It seems innocent by comparison, doesn't it? Anyway, I'm sorry I dragged you into this, I promise it wasn't intentional."

We cleaned up the main entry way first. Scarlet threw as much of it away as she could.

"I almost feel like the burglar did me a favor," she laughed. "If only they'd do this to the whole house, I wouldn't have to have a garage sale!"

She closed the closet door and tied up the garbage bag.

"I'll take that."

"Thanks. I don't want to hurt my stupid back again. I'll show you where to drop it."

We went to the backyard and Scarlet pointed to the far side of the detached garage. I found a couple of battered metal bins and stuffed the garbage into one of them. As I turned, I saw two cars pulling into the driveway.

If Ford ever made a car called the Unmarked, I bet it would be a bestseller. There was no doubt who it was. Two men came out of each vehicle. One of them held up a badge.

"Scarlet Brennan?"

"Yes?"

"We'd like to ask you a few questions."

One of the detectives turned to me. "And you are?"

"Bert Shambles."

The cops glanced at each other.

"Ms. Brennan, could we speak to you inside, please?"

"Of course. Right this way."

They started for the house. I started to go too, but the other two detectives stopped me.

"Just a moment. We'd like to speak to you out here."

"Okay."

"Mind telling us where you were last night?"

"I was here in the afternoon, then at the Knights of Columbus hall for a party, then at my place overnight."

"Can anybody corroborate that?"

"I was with Scarlet the whole time."

"Anyone else?"

"Her friend China was with us for part of it."

"Which part?"

"They both stayed over at my place last night."

"Both? Why, was it a late night?"

"Not really. We were just eager to get to bed."

"So when you say they stayed with you, do you mean they stayed in a guest room, or on a pull-out couch or something?"

"No, my bed."

"You and her and her friend stayed in your bed last night? What time did they leave?"

"Around eight this morning."

"That's pretty early after being at a party the night before. Any reason they were in a hurry?"

"China needed to get back to her yoga studio to teach a class. Plus, she had to get all the video equipment back, so she could finish editing."

"I see. What did you do then?"

"I ran after my girlfriend. Or ex-girlfriend, I should say."

"Who is that, Scarlet?"

"No, another woman. She showed up at my place unexpectedly and got upset. I had to explain it to her."

"I'm sure you did."

"Let me get this straight," the other detective said. "You had this lady and another woman in bed last night, and your girlfriend found you in the morning and got upset?"

"Yes. She just doesn't understand."

"I should think not."

"It's not what it sounds like."

"It never is," he sighed. He reached into a folder and pulled out a sheet of paper. It was a photograph. It looked like an official evidence photo, judging by the letters and words at the bottom. It was a mug shot of Prince Shieldhart.

"You ever seen this before?"

"That's Prince Shieldhart!" I cried. "I lost him last night!"

"Do you remember where you lost him?"

"In the Phowl bus, after the party."

"What were you doing there?"

"I was looking for a friend of Scarlet's, Brent."

"Did you have an appointment with him or something?"

"She did, but he never showed. So I went in to find him."

"Did you?"

"No, it was too dark and the Night Vision potion didn't work. Why?"

"Please turn around."

"Excuse me?"

"I said, please turn around."

I felt the cold steel snap against one wrist, then the other.

"Look, I understand that you have to do your job," I said. "But I think wasting taxpayer dollars to solve The Case of the Missing D&D figurine is freaking ridiculous."

"This isn't about the figurine. It's about a suspicious death."

"I had nothing to do with Gavin's electrocution," I said. "I was as shocked as anyone. Okay, bad choice of words."

"This isn't about Gavin. It's about the death of Brent Turlock. We found your little friend on his body last night."

"Very clumsy of you," said the other. "Very, very clumsy."

CHAPTER 18: AT THE STATION

They led me into the station. Arnie was sitting behind the front desk. He jumped to his feet when he saw me.

"I knew we were going to nail you eventually! I told you!"

"Stuff it, O'Toole," one of the detectives barked. "If you got nothing better to do, I'll find something for you."

Arnie muttered an apology and sat back down and started shuffling papers. I was led downstairs. The cuffs were removed and I was put into a holding cell.

I wanted to call my mom, but I wouldn't unless it was absolutely necessary. She works for a local attorney, who'd gotten me out of a jam once before. I didn't want to ask for his help again. To say nothing of the hard time my mom would give me. She wasn't too thrilled when the details of my adventure over the summer became public. She blamed Aria for my troubles, even though Aria had nothing to do with any of it. My mom called her "that Mafioso's daughter" and other such names. When I asked her what she had against Aria, she said her dad usually parked in one of the handicapped spaces in front of St. Boniface for Sunday mass, even though he didn't have a permit.

I sat for more than an hour. Then one of the detectives—I'd say the one with the bad-fitting clothes, the mustache, and the pot belly, but that described all of them—took me out of the cell and led me to a windowless interrogation room. I was hoping it would have one of those two-way mirrors like on TV, but there were only a few small cameras mounted in the corners. The detective who led me in—I think it was Aronson—was joined by the other guy, Orozco.

"You're quite a ladies' man, aren't you?"

"No, sir."

"Don't be modest. Two women spend the night, your girlfriend finds you. Any of that have any bearing on why Brent Turlock was murdered last night, and why we found your little figurine on his dead body?"

"Is that like your calling card?" the other one asked. "Should we call you the D&D Killer?"

"That's good," the other one chuckled.

"I swear, I didn't know he was in there. I called his name and tried seeing into the van, but it was too dark."

"So how did your little figurine wind up there?"

"I don't know; it was in my hand and must have dropped."

"How long have you been friends with Scarlet Brennan?"

"We just met a couple of days ago."

"I see. How about her friend, China?"

"Same."

"Don't you think it's strange," Orozco said, "that two women would be sleeping over at your place after you've only known them a couple of days?"

"Especially considering how crummy your place is," Aronson said. "We went by there first, before we found you at Miss Brennan's. Pretty destitute, if you ask me."

"I'm surprised two beautiful women like them would be interested in a guy like you."

"It's not what you think. Nothing happened between us. We just needed a place to crash."

"Scarlet's house looks nice. Why didn't you stay there?"

"We went over to China's place after the party."

"Why didn't you stay there?"

"She said her place had been broken into, and that there were some suspicious characters hanging around outside her building."

"Really? Why didn't she call the police?"

"She felt silly, like maybe she was just being paranoid."

"We respond to calls like that all the time. We don't mind. You don't think there was a reason why she didn't want to call us?"

"I honestly don't know."

"Okay. So after you pick her up, what then? You just all decided to go to your fleabag of a place, instead of Scarlet's beautiful, clean home?"

"Speaking of clean, what were you putting into the trash when we arrived?"

"I was helping her clean up."

"Evidence?"

"No, stuff that was broken when her place got broken into."

"Her place was broken into? I thought you said China's place was."

"It was. They both were."

"And you don't find that suspicious?"

"Of course I do! Who wouldn't find break-ins suspicious?"

"I mean, it wasn't suspicious to you that neither of them called the police to report either incident?"

"You'll have to ask them about that."

"We're asking you, wise guy."

The door to the interrogation room opened and Arnie stuck his head in. Aronson turned. "Yeah?"

"Sir, could I please have a word with you?" He had a look and a tone in his voice that it was important. I noticed he didn't look so cocky as before, which made me feel a little better, since I could pretty much guarantee that his mood would get better the worse I was treated, and sadder if things started going my way. It gave me hope.

Aronson went outside, with Arnie. Orozco didn't say anything, just kept staring at me. A minute later Aronson came back in and asked Orozco to come outside, too. The three of them stood there, with the door partly propped open. I couldn't hear what they were saying but at some point Orozco cursed and hit the door. Then he stalked off. Aronson opened the door fully and glared at me.

"You didn't tell me you had such powerful friends."

"I don't know what you mean."

"Of course, you don't. Okay, we're done here. You can go."

"Really?"

"Are you deaf? I said get out of here. Officer O'Toole will bring you upstairs." As I went past Aronson he added, "Let me give you some advice. If you're covering for either of those women, or lying or withholding any information from us, next time your friends won't be able to help you."

Arnie didn't say a word on the way upstairs. Not a smirk, not a smart remark, not a veiled threat. He was the model of professionalism. Whatever was going on, it had scared him straight. As we approached the desk, I saw a man standing there. The light streaming in from the front doors of the stationhouse made him look more like a silhouette, until I got closer.

It was my mom's boss, Mr. Barbarino.

His business card says, Vincent J. Barbarino, Esq., but my mom calls him "Vinnie Barbarino" and giggles every time she says it. Something about an old TV show, that's all I know. I call him Mr. Barbarino. He had represented me for free during my earlier trouble with the law, and had done a great job.

I thought about what I'd tell them. I decided I'd be completely open and honest and tell them everything, with just a few exceptions. I couldn't tell them about the Far Out; Daddy-O would find out about that soon enough, when my urine test came back. I also didn't want to mention the Wheels chasing us, or me stealing Prince Shieldhart, or Scarlet stealing the drugs from her ex-housemate. Okay, maybe there were a lot of things I didn't want to tell them.

The door to the cell opened.

"Can I call my mom now?"

"You can call whoever you like. You're free to go."

Mr. Barbarino was standing by the front desk. He was wearing a Hawaiian shirt that was opened at the top, revealing a lot of gold and chest hair, loose-fitting white linen pants, and brown leather sandals. His face was a different story: he had a serious expression that was completely at odds with the bright, easygoing outfit. He addressed me as Mr. Shambles and shook my hand with both hands. When he talked to the guy behind the desk, he referred to me as "my client." My client this, my client that. Mr. Barbarino escorted me out.

"I'm really sorry you had to bother with this," I said. "I can't tell you how much I appreciate it."

"I know you do, Mr. Shambles. It was my pleasure. Here is my car."

It was a big Cadillac, black and sporty looking.

"I guess Scarlet must have called my mom," I said. "I was waiting to use the phone so I could ask her to call you."

"Your mother did not call me. My services were retained by another individual."

"Who? Scarlet?"

"No. It was Mr. Tortura who called me."

"Mr. Tortura? I've never even met him."

"He finds it advantageous to his business interests to keep apprised of what is happening around town, however unrelated to those interests it may at first appear."

Mr. Tortura is Aria's father. He's supposedly a tough character with a shady past. I couldn't believe it. My mom had worked for Mr. Barbarino for many years, pretty much ever since my dad left twenty years ago, but I hadn't known until that moment that he was a mob lawyer. I wondered if she knew.

The silence in the car felt awkward, so I tried filling it with small talk.

"But why would Mr. Tortura care what happens to me?"

Mr. Barbarino smiled.

"My client is aware of your brave actions over the summer. He wanted to find a way to express his gratitude for saving his daughter's life."

"Of course," I said. "I'm very grateful to you both."

"Thank you. I will convey your sentiments to my client."

"Am I completely free and clear?"

"Yes. They made some noises about minor charges for menacing and theft, but I will take care of it. It's nothing to worry about. My sources tell me that the body in the van had been dead for at least twelve hours."

"That must be why it smelled so bad in there."

"I am not an expert on the decomposition characteristics of the human body; however, I think you may be correct in that assumption."

I couldn't imagine the level of influence Mr. Tortura had, that he could get me sprung so quickly. It was as impressive as it was scary.

We pulled up to Scarlet's house. I shook hands with Mr. Barbarino.

"Thank you again."

"It was my pleasure. Before you go, there's one more thing. Mr. Tortura also requests, now that he has repaid his debt to you—that you will refrain from dating his daughter in the future."

A lump formed in my throat. My heart filled like a water balloon and dropped down to my shoes and went splat.

"Tell Mr. Tortura that I have no plans to see his daughter ever again."

"Thank you. I shall convey your message."

I got out of the Cadillac and watched as Mr. Barbarino drove off. So that was it. The rich always closed ranks. It wasn't a mob thing, it wasn't an Italian thing; in the end it was always about money. It made the situation between Aria and me more real somehow. Final. I knew I should be relieved but my insides ached.

I turned and saw Scarlet, standing in the open doorway. I dragged myself up the walk and she hugged me.

"Pretty fancy taxi service you use. What's wrong? You look terrible."

"I feel terrible."

"Me too. I've been so upset, between the news about Brent and then the thought that you were going to be accused. I didn't know what to do."

"It's all right. They don't really think of me as a suspect, they were just looking for information."

"Who dropped you off?"

"My lawyer."

"You are a man of mystery, Bert Shambles. No offense, but you don't strike me as a guy who has a lawyer, let alone a lawyer with a Cadillac who acts as a car service."

"It surprises me too sometimes."

We went inside. Scarlet had cleaned up the mess in the front entryway.

"Do you want something to eat or drink?"

"I'm starving."

"You're in luck. I just made some veggie burgers. I was so nervous I needed something to do."

We went into the kitchen. I sat at the table while Scarlet busied herself at the counter.

"So I learned a couple of interesting things," she said. "First, I think I know why the police don't consider you a suspect. They told me that Brent had most likely been killed earlier, and then was driven to that spot."

"I wonder why."

"Me too, and that relates to the second thing that they told me. Brent's cellphone wasn't found."

"But he texted you."

"Someone texted me. But it wasn't him."

"Why?"

"I don't know, but I have a few theories. First, I thought it was probably a ruse, to get me out of the house and to the Knights of Columbus hall so whoever was texting me could break into my house."

"Why take all that risk and make it so complicated?"

"Exactly. It doesn't make sense. Then I remembered something else. It seemed so minor and insignificant at the time that I didn't even think of it until I was talking to the detectives. I saw someone, when I was waiting for Brent by the back door of the K of C hall. It was right after the lights went out. A guy came out of a side door. He was wearing one of those crazy costumes, like an Orc or a Dwarf."

"Maybe he was a combination of both. A Dorc."

"Ha! That's good; I'll remember that. No, this guy was different. I mean, he had on a costume but there was something about the way he carried himself, just the energy he gave off. I remember feeling creeped out by him, like an evil vibe. He was walking down the hallway towards me. I hoped he was going to just go past me and out the back door." She shuddered. "The more I think about it the more creeped out I get."

"What happened? Did he say anything to you?"

"No, because one of the other costumed guys came running down the hall and said that there was a riot, that they needed his help. The scary guy cursed and shoved past me out the back door. It was one of those doors with a panic bar, connected to an alarm, but because the electricity was shut off the alarm didn't work. That's when I ran back and found you, and we took off."

"There's something else," I said. "You're not going to like it."

"What?"

"You talked to Brent yesterday afternoon, right?"

"Yeah. It was like four or five, I think. So he must have been killed between then and when I got the texts."

I shook my head.

"Mr. Barbarino told me that Brent had been dead for at least twelve hours by the time he was found. That means whoever called you was only pretending to be Brent."

"So whoever it was on the phone just wanted me to go down to the K of C hall. But why?" Her expression dropped. "You don't think they were after me, do you?"

"It's a possibility we have to consider."

"Oh, man."

Scarlet closed her eyes and did some deep breathing. Then she straightened herself up and looked at me with a strange expression.

"It just occurred to me. If someone really was trying to kill me, they probably would have succeeded if you hadn't started that riot."

"Don't thank me; thank Prince Shieldhart."

She held up two plates. "To Prince Shieldhart!"

Scarlet sat down and we ate. The veggie burgers were like her lemonade, made from scratch and ridiculously good.

We ate in silence. Then I took the plates to the dishwasher and wiped down the table. Scarlet stood up and stretched, pulling one leg up behind her back, then the other.

"Okay, so we've determined that I'm very likely the target of a homicidal maniac. I'll understand if you want to run away and never see me again. That's what I'd do if I were you."

"Not a chance. I think it's time we paid Martin Douglas a visit."

"He definitely wasn't the guy I saw in the hallway."

"I know, but he's still involved in this up to his axe-hole," I said. "That reminds me of something."

"What?"

I shook it off. "Never mind; it's gone. Come on, I'll drive."

CHAPTER 19: NOT THE NOT THIN MAN

Rosemary & Time Nostalgia Shoppe was in a historic building on lower Main Street, set back from the road behind a large gravel yard, around the corner from the Town Dock. I turned off Main a few blocks early.

"Why are you going this way?"

"I can take Bayview down to Main, then turn right. That way I won't have to turn against oncoming traffic. He might see us that way."

"Maintaining the element of surprise? I'm impressed, Bert Shambles. You really do know what you're doing."

I pulled into the gravel yard that served as a parking lot, in front of the shop. It was an old barn-like structure that was probably a carriage house at one time. It was painted a deep red. I reached to turn off the engine but Scarlet put her hand on mine and stopped me.

"Don't bother. It's closed."

The lights were off and a big CLOSED sign hung in the window. Next to it there was a sign with store hours.

"Can you read that?"

"It's supposed to be open, 10-5. Let me check around back."

Scarlet got out of the Olds and jogged to the far rear edge of the building. Then she turned and waved me over. I shut off the engine and got out of the Olds and joined her.

"He can't be very far. Look."

There was a space behind the shop, partially obscured by overgrown bushes that were hanging down over a retaining wall. A dirty tarp covered a small car that was parked there. Scarlet pulled back the corner of the tarp.

"Look familiar?"

It was a small red Hyundai, the same make and model that Martin was driving when he tried running me down. I examined the right tire. It was scratched and scraped.

"That's Martin's car all right. It even has the damage where he hit the curb instead of me."

"Where would he go without a car? He doesn't look like the walking type."

"He might have gone up the street to the deli. There are a bunch of places to eat around here that he might have walked to."

I put my hand on the hood of the car, like I'd seen on TV.

"It's cold."

"What does that mean?"

"That it hasn't been driven in a while."

"Is that important?"

"I have no idea."

Just then something caught my eye. Movement in the second floor window over the store. I looked but only saw a curtain moving.

"Did you see that?"

"What?"

"Someone was at that window. I think he's hiding from us."

"Do you think he knew we were coming? You were so careful coming in the way you did."

"I don't know. Maybe we're not the only people he's hiding from."

Scarlet sighed.

"I don't know about you, but I'm tired and I want to get home and finish cleaning up the mess. It's been a really upsetting couple of days. The last thing I want to do is play cat and mouse with an overgrown baby."

Maybe it was my own delayed response to everything that had happened, but something about the situation suddenly made me very angry.

"No. I'm not leaving until I've confronted that s.o.b. I've been arrested, locked in a cell, and accused of possibly killing a keyboardist. I've been drugged, chased by bikers, shot at by Orcs, slapped, and accused of having orgies. I've been forced to pee in a cup and drink liquefied bat wings. Not only that, but it turns out that my mom's boss is a mob lawyer, who made me promise never to talk to the love of my life ever again. So I am not, under any circumstances, going to let some costume-wearing, forty-year-old virgin toy collector get the better of me. And if you have any problems with that, you can just wiggle your hippie butt out of here, because it's Shambles' time."

"Wow," Scarlet said, "You must be a riot in the sack."

"Thank you."

I marched over to the Hyundai and stepped onto the hood, leaving a nice dent in it, and onto the roof. It was a bit of a reach to the lower roof but there was a downspout that had just enough stability to pull myself up with, though it broke away from the side in a couple of places. I got one knee onto the edge and pulled myself up the rest of the way.

"Be careful of your arm!" Scarlet called to me. "Don't take any unnecessary risks."

My arm was fine, as long as I didn't do anything stupid—which, I had to admit, breaking into a business might be considered. I walked like a tightrope walker up the steep slope and grabbed onto the edge of a windowsill and peered in. There was a small room, crammed with boxes and papers. The window was old but had extra reinforcements—a metal bar, and a couple of those things they stick to windows when they alarm them.

"Anything?"

"No. The place's alarmed, though."

"You think? It might just be a fake. I can't see a guy like Martin investing in something like an alarm system."

"Do you want me to risk it?"

"No, better not."

"I'll go around to the other side. Hold on."

"Be careful, Burt. I'm really worried. It's a long drop."

I looked. It wasn't too bad, but behind the car were old metal pieces and broken glass.

I had to take another step up, to the intermediate level. This was trickier, and a loose nail caught me on the hand, leaving a nice hole in my palm.

"Are you all right?"

"Fine. I'm almost there."

"I'm going to see if there's a doorbell or something. He's got to open eventually."

I got up to the next level and caught my breath before inching around to the back. There was another window, but the branches of an unruly maple tree were pressed tight against the corner of the building. The guy really needed some basic landscaping done. Maybe I could get him to hire me when it was all over.

"Hey!" Scarlet yelled from the front of the house, out of sight. "The front door's unlocked!"

Of course it was. Now all I had to do was get myself back down without killing myself in the process. I saw a better way down, by hanging from one of the branches of the tree, swinging my leg onto the retaining wall behind the building, then letting go just enough to turn and grab onto the edge of the lower roof. It wasn't exactly parkour, but I managed to do it without further injury.

I landed behind the red Hyundai. The space was so narrow that I had to climb over the car to get back out and around to the front. The door was open a few inches. I went in.

It was dark inside, but my eyes adjusted quickly. There were old toys everywhere; comics in bags hanging from the moldings, boxes of albums and magazines. It seemed like a cool store; it was a shame it was owned by such a jerk. I looked over and saw Scarlet, standing very still in the middle of the room, near the register. There was a scruffy-looking guy behind the counter.

"Is Martin here?" I asked.

"Bert—"

"Don't move, man. I don't want to hurt you."

That's when I noticed the scruffy guy was holding a gun.

"Hey, if you're robbing the place we'll gladly give you a hand," I said. "We hate the owner."

"Bert, this is Peter, my ex-housemate. The guy who made Far Out."

"You made Far Out?"

Pete nodded. "Yeah, so what?"

"It's pretty freaking amazing, dude. You're really talented."

"Thank you. But if you take one more step I'm going to kill you."

I looked at his eyes and knew he was serious. Even worse, he had a look in his eyes that I'd only ever seen before in the expressions of the people I sometimes found on my front lawn, babbling about UFOs or trying to give me a copy of *The Watchtower*. He looked paranoid, burned-out, desperate.

"Pete, let my friend go. He has nothing to do with this."

"He just said how much he liked my work. No way. Neither of you are going anywhere."

"And do what? Kill us over some missing drugs? Who would even do that?"

"Don't you watch the news? Happens every day. It's one of the most common things people kill each other over."

"I gotta agree with Pete on that," I said.

"You're not helping."

"You owe me a lot of money, and I'm not leaving until I get it."

"It's not like I have thousands of dollars in my pocket that I can just hand over," Scarlet cried. "I'll need time to pull that kind of cash together."

"I don't want money; I want this."

Pete pulled something out of his back pocket and threw it at her. She unfolded a black and white photograph of four guys standing around in a park next to a tree. They were all wearing hippie clothes. "The Peppermint Wristwatch" was printed in bubble letters at the bottom. The picture was riddled with small holes. Next to that it said, "Martin" and a phone number. I recognized the handwriting as Scarlet's, from the Phestival phlyer—I mean flyer—she gave me.

"You want a picture of her dad's band?" I asked. "That's crazy."

Scarlet shot me a look. "You mean it's not a common reason for people to kill each other?" she asked.

"Cut the clowning. I want what's in your dad's hands."

I leaned over and looked. Nobody was holding anything except for the one guy holding a guitar.

"You want a guitar?"

"That's right. You give it to me and I won't hurt you."

"Pete, you have to believe me. I have no idea about any guitars. The only guitars my dad had around were a couple of acoustic folk guitars that me and my brother tried learning how to play. But if you want them, sure, be my guest."

"That's not what Gavin thought. That's not what Martin thinks."

"Where is Martin?"

"I'm tired of everyone betraying me. It's not going to happen again."

"Nobody's betraying you. Please, let's talk this over."

"No. You think you're smooth like silk but you're rough like sand. You're all trying to keep me from getting my share. I ought to blow your head off right now."

"I swear I have no idea what you're talking about. Yes, I took your drugs. I'm sorry. I was mad at you, but I wasn't trying to cheat you. I was trying to keep you from giving yourself permanent brain damage."

"You're saying I make bad stuff?"

"No! Not that I know, but I've heard it's very good."

"Trust me, it's awesome," I said.

"But that's just it. Maybe it's too good. If anything it's too powerful."

"That's because nobody has the intellect or the spirituality to grasp it." Tears were streaming down his face. "You just don't get it."

"What happened with Gavin? Why did you say he was involved?"

"He came back to Bangor a few weeks ago, during a break in the summer tour. Even though I hated his guts, Gav was my best customer over the years; he must have moved ten thousand doses at shows. Except I didn't have any more, because you'd stolen my whole stash and I had no money to make more. I told him what you'd done. I'd put your picture up on my dart board and was using it for practice. Gav saw that picture and he freaked out."

"Why? Did he say?"

"No, he just snapped a picture of it with his phone and split. I finally decided to call the number on the picture and I talked to Martin. He wouldn't tell me much, but I finally pieced enough together that I understood what was going down. He and Gav were working together to cheat you, get the guitar for very cheap and then keep all the money for themselves."

"I don't believe it. Gavin wouldn't have cheated me. He and I were friends."

"So were Gavin and me. So were me and you. Look how that turned out."

"What do those bikers have to do with this?" I asked.

"Everything, man. They fronted the money for the supplies and equipment. Some pretty expensive stuff. Did Scarlet tell you that she also smashed it all? I didn't think so. That was a few grand right there. The Wheels found ways of getting the more difficult ingredients, no problem. It wouldn't have been possible without their support, and they knew it. They owned me."

"I couldn't sit by and watch you descend into hell," Scarlet said. "It made me sick, watching you all play that whole Breaking Bad and Sons of Anarchy stuff. You used to be a poet, man, a light of inspiration in a dark world! Not a drug dealer." Scarlet started sobbing. I tried putting my arm around her but Pete jabbed the gun at me and I backed off.

"I told them what you did. Know what they said? They didn't care; said it was my fault for not getting rid of you sooner, for trusting you. They gave me until the end of the summer tour to get it figured out and a new batch made or they were going to kill me and hide my body where no one would ever find it. That's what they said."

"So how does the guitar fit into this?"

"I told Gavin what had happened, since he knows you and he works with the Wheels. He said he'd loan me the money to get me back in business, and keep the Wheels off my back. He's made a lot of money off my product; it basically financed Phowl during their hard times. But he said he'd only do it if I did a job for him. I had to break into your house and steal that guitar."

"So you broke in, even after he died?"

"I never did it. I was supposed to during the Phestival, then I got a text from Martin that Gavin had died."

"You were all in on it together?"

"It doesn't feel good being betrayed by friends, does it?"

"Did Brent know about the plan?"

"He knew something was up. He saw me before the Phestival, and he knew what a schemer Gav was. I don't know how much else he knows."

"You mean *knew*," I corrected him. "Brent's dead."

"What? No way. Oh, man, no way."

He reached into a front pocket with a free hand and pulled out a vial. He flipped the cap with his thumb, held the vial under his nose and inhaled deeply.

"Don't do that to yourself. Don't do any more harm to your brain."

"Don't knock it 'til you've tried it, babe. This is the new and improved Far Out. You inhale it. Instant rush, totally amazing."

"I don't believe Gavin would have cheated me, or had you break into my house."

"Really? That's what you think. He called the number on the picture and got in touch with Martin and made a deal with him. They were working together to cheat you. But he wasn't careful—no no no! He flew too close to the sun and his wings melted. Bzzzt bzzzt bzzzt!" Pete held his arms out and jerked like he was being electrocuted.

"So you killed him because of some stupid memorabilia? You tampered with his amplifier?"

"No way, man; it wasn't me, wasn't me, wasn't me. I couldn't have gotten near that scene, the Wheels and the band all know me. No, no; it was the leather man."

"What leather man? Do you mean Lizard, or one of the other Wheels? They wear a lot of leather."

"Not leather clothes, ha ha! You're so silly, Scarlet. I mean the Leatherman, like the tool! Sort of like a Swiss Army knife, but better. He's the master of disaster, the man with the plan. Said he was just going to send Gav a message, but I guess the message was louder and clearer than he expected."

"What are you talking about?"

"Incense and peppermint," Pete sing-songed. "Incense and peppermint. The kitty-cat has come back for his flower. The kitty-cat has come back for his flower."

"His mind's fried," Scarlet said to me. "Sampling too much of his own product."

"I'm so glad I overdosed on his drugs," I said.

"I'm not so crazy that I can't blow your heads off right now," he said.

"Haven't you killed enough people?" I asked. "First Gavin, then Brent."

"That wasn't me; it was the kitty-cat coming back for his flower. Kitty-cat doesn't like loose ends. He's got claws."

There was a sound of tires on gravel. A car pulled up to the front of the store. It was a police car.

CHAPTER 20: ATTICS OF YOUR MIND

"Get rid of them," Pete said. "Don't tell them anything or I'll let them know all about your drug-stealing ways, Scarlet. And don't forget I have the gun."

Pete slipped through a door behind the counter, out of sight. He left the door open a crack.

"I can see both of you from here," he said in a low tone.

A cop got out of the passenger side and peered through the window. He pushed open the door. It was Arnie O'Toole.

"Hello? What's going on in here? Oh, it's you, Shambles. I should have known. Why are the lights off? What are you doing here?"

"We came in to talk to the owner," Scarlet said sweetly. "The door was unlocked, I swear. We thought maybe he was in the bathroom or something."

"We got a call that someone was on the roof, appeared to be trying to break in. That wouldn't have been you by any chance, was it?"

"Why would you think it was me?" I asked.

"For one thing, you're holding your hands up."

It was true. My arms were still raised in surrender. I lowered them.

"Honestly, officer," Scarlet continued quickly, "we only just got here a minute ago, and wondered the same things you're wondering, like why nobody's here when the sign in the window clearly states the store should be open now."

"You can make your statements at the station."

Arnie lifted his radio. Just then a car roared by, spitting gravel. Arnie's partner came into the store.

"That was our perp," he said. "He must have had a car parked in back. Red Hyundai."

Arnie cursed. He glared at me.

"You better be available to answer some questions later."

He and his partner ran out. The lights and siren went on and the cruiser spun out of the lot.

"He must have climbed down the way I went up," I said. "Someone must have seen me on the roof and called the police, and now they think it's him."

"Good riddance. I just hope he doesn't try going out in a blaze of glory and start shooting."

"I don't think that'll be necessary."

I went behind the counter, through the open door. There were stairs leading to the second floor. The gun was lying on a step about halfway up. I picked it up carefully by the barrel. It was an old revolver. It had fancy script on the side. The script said "Roy Rogers." I pointed it at the wall and pulled the trigger. *Bang*, went the revolver.

"It's a cap gun. Let's get out of here."

"What about the store? Where's Martin?"

"Pete obviously had his keys and had driven the car here. Which means that either he and Martin are working together, or else—"

"Or else what? Oh, no. Don't say it. You don't think so?"

We both looked up at the ceiling.

"There's only one way to find out," I said.

There was a lot of junk upstairs: boxes of extra inventory, a cluttered shipping station with a scale and postage machine, a wire basket overflowing with receipts, orders, and bills. But no dead body, no Martin.

The only thing we found was a sleeping bag in the corner of one room, with a little battery-powered camping lantern, an inflatable pillow and a backpack with some clothes. Scarlet picked up a T-shirt, with "Bangor Bar & Grill" printed on it.

"This is one of Pete's. He was crashing here."

I saw a wire sticking out from under a sheet. I pulled out an iPhone.

"He forgot his phone." I swiped the screen but a keypad came up, asking for a PIN. "It's locked."

"Try 7-1-7-1."

I punched in the numbers. The screen unlocked.

"How'd you know that?"

"I lived with the guy, remember? I helped him set that phone up."

I slipped it into my back pocket.

"The cops might need this," I said. "This place is giving me the creeps. Let's get out of here."

"What about the store?"

"What about it?"

"Do we just leave it open? Someone could just walk in and steal everything."

"You're worried about the possessions of a guy who tried stealing from you?"

"You're right. Let's go."

Scarlet stared at the photograph during the ride back.

"This was the band's only publicity photo that I know of. I'd never even seen it before, until after my dad passed away. I found it in his desk, in the upstairs study, and made some copies of it."

"So how did it end up in Maine?"

"It was such a crazy time for me. I still had most of my stuff up there, I was still on the fence about whether I'd want to keep living there and just come down here to clean up my dad's estate, or if I wanted to break my ties with the scene in Maine and start fresh down here.

It wasn't too hard of a decision, though it was still really hard to do. Pete was just too far gone, the Wheels were always hanging around, the band was always on the road, people were just into partying and getting high and watching TV. I just felt like, if you want to stay young and idealistic and keep having fun, fine. But just getting stoned and watching cartoons isn't being young, it's infantile. And there's nothing older than an infantile adult. Sorry, that must sound really preachy. I loved those guys, loved Pete and that crazy scene, but after a certain age if you're not careful, a darkness sets in, a creeping cynicism or bitterness that sneaks up on people. I've seen it happen a lot."

"So what's the escape from that? What's the antidote?"

"Just facing your responsibilities, for one thing. You can't let them rule you but you have to face them and deal with them. I also think you need to set a few longer-term plans, whether it's to create something, or achieve something, have a career or whatever. It could be writing novels or painting, or starting a family or a farm, having a business like Chi's yoga studio. Something to ground you and give you a new set of skills in life, teach you how to relate to people in different and more meaningful ways. I don't know, I'm just babbling."

We got back to Scarlet's and went into the living room. Scarlet turned on the stereo, sifted through some CDs sitting next to it, picked one and put it in the player and pressed *play*.

"I miss those days, though; I have to be honest. We had a lot of good times. Pete was really awesome before he got into drugs."

"What are we listening to?"

"It's Phowl's first album, when Pete was still with them. This is him singing. Didn't he have a nice voice?"

There was a lot of energy in the music, fast chord changes, rapid-fire drum fills and bass lines. Two guitars squawked at each other in a call and response; a big wobbly organ sound swooshed and sloshed around it all. It sounded like they were having fun. Pete started singing:

Seek beyond material things
and freedom you will find
Seal your disappointment in
the attics of your mind!

"Do you like it?"

"It's okay. The lyrics are kind of corny."

"My dad wrote them."

"Ouch. Sorry."

"It's okay; I like honesty. You're right; they are corny. They were modern for the 1960s, though. My dad helped produce the first Phowl album, because I'd come home from college just raving about how great they were. He liked their demo and offered to help them in the studio for free."

"That was nice of him."

"Wasn't it? That's the kind of guy my dad was. It helped the band get on a bigger label, get their start in the business. They recorded one of his old Peppermint Wristwatch songs as a tribute, to thank him."

We listened to the end of the song. Scarlet sighed.

"I always wondered if that's what he did."

"What?"

"Sealed his disappointment away, where it couldn't hurt him. He lost his band and the woman he loved. A lot of his rock star friends died, like Janis and Jimi,

Pigpen and countless others. The scene evaporated, the 60s turned into the 70s, with Vietnam dragging on and Watergate, the oil crisis and all that. I can understand why some people weren't able to deal with it, but I'm really glad he adapted and changed, grew with the times. I can't imagine how much pain he must have been in. And yet he never made me and my brother feel anything except how loved we were."

"Maybe he covered all that pain too well. Anything that was sealed in the attics of his mind are buried with him now. Unless there's something in the attic here."

"No, there's no attic, I checked. Which is strange, because we have a pretty high, slanted roof. You'd think there'd be something up there, a crawlspace at least."

"You sure there isn't?"

"I've checked. There's no door or other way up there. There's nothing."

"Just because there's no door, doesn't mean there's nothing," I said.

"That's a very deep thought, Bert Shambles. I think my dad would have liked you, you two think alike in a lot of ways." Her expression dropped and she stared at me. "Are you thinking what I'm thinking?"

"That depends. Are you thinking about a chicken cutlet sandwich?"

"No, the attic."

"You said there isn't one."

"I said there's no door. You're a genius. Follow me."

Scarlet opened a drawer and took out a flashlight, then led me up to the second floor, into the small den where Pete broke in—or didn't break in, if his drugged-out ramblings were to be believed. The mess of boxes were still spilling out of the closet.

"Can you give me a hand with these?"

Scarlet handed the boxes to me, and I stacked them into any available spaces.

"What is all this stuff?"

"Everything. A lot of it has to do with his advertising work. Lots of notebooks, tapes, discs, files. He was such a pack rat, but growing up I thought advertising was his whole life. When I found out more about his past, when I was a teenager, he would hardly talk about it. He always said he had nothing left from that time. But someone like my dad, who liked to save everything, couldn't have just thrown it all away."

"So what are we looking for?"

"I'll show you. Here's the last box."

I took the box and stacked it with the rest. Scarlet navigated the desk chair through the boxes and into the closet and stood on it.

"Hand me the flashlight, please."

I gave it to her. She shined it at the ceiling closet. There was water staining, brown splotches, and some bubbling plaster down the top part of the wall. A strip of sheetrock tape was visible in the ceiling where it partially separated from the panel.

"There was a roof leak a few years back. My dad got it fixed, but it caused some water damage in this closet. He never fixed the interior, though, and it makes me wonder..." She pointed the flashlight at the opposite corner of the den. "There's a broom over there. Can you bring it to me?"

I did as she asked and handed her the broom. She gave me the flashlight.

"Point the beam up here, in the ceiling. Perfect."

I held the flashlight steady as Scarlet flipped the broom over. She poked the ceiling and some bits of plaster came down and clattered on the floor.

"Do you see a door?"

"Nope. Guess we'll just have to make one."

She rammed the broom handle up. There was a crunch, and a lot of plaster and sheetrock fell to the ground.

"What are you doing?"

"Heck, this would have to be fixed before I put the house on the market to sell. Might as well make the most of it."

Scarlet scrunched her face and closed her eyes, then jammed the broom up into the ceiling, again and again. Dust and pieces of ceiling crumbled and fell.

"Almost there. This is actually kind of fun."

She rammed and poked some more. Then she handed me the broom and stood on her toes and reached up. There was a final cracking sound and more dust.

"Ta-da!"

Scarlet pulled her hand down, with a big chunk of sheetrock in her hand.

"I think there's enough room to work with. But we're going to need a ladder."

"I can grab the one from outside."

I ran downstairs and out back, got the ladder and carefully maneuvered it up to the den. Scarlet had moved the chair; together we got the ladder into the closet. It was a tight, awkward fit, but we stabilized it.

"I'll go," I said. "Can't let you have all the fun."

"You sure?"

I went up the ladder and worked my torso through the opening. Then I ducked back down.

"Light."

She handed me the flashlight and I went back up. It was a small attic, musty and stuffy. I turned to the right because it was easier to move my body that way. I saw the roof beams and lots of insulation, but nothing else.

"Anything?"

"Not yet. I have to shift."

"Be careful."

I turned my body slowly to the left and trained the light the other way. In the far corner I saw a small metal rack, like the kind they hang clothes on. There were several garment bags hanging on it. Underneath, I saw a couple of suitcases.

"There's something here," I said. "Looks like we found some of your dad's old clothes and luggage."

"No," said Scarlet. "I think we've found the attic of his mind."

CHAPTER 21 THE MAGIC AXE

I pulled myself up through the hole and onto the struts, then helped Scarlet into the attic. There were some planks laid across the beams that led to a few large pieces of paneling that acted as a sort of floor. Scarlet opened the first suitcase.

"These must be some of my dad's old stage clothes. Point the beam over here."

She picked up a few shirts and a pair of pants.

"This stuff is amazing! It's not in great shape, but it looks really cool."

Underneath the clothes there was a portfolio, the kind that artists sometimes use, with a cloth string tying it together. Scarlet untied the ribbon and opened it.

I might not know exactly what things are worth, but I've seen Antiques Roadshow enough times to know when something looks really valuable. This stuff all had that look: there were concert posters signed by the artists who appeared; a drunken note from Janis Joplin, making lewd suggestions to Scarlet's dad; a set list that was probably personally written by Jimi Hendrix; finally Scarlet picked up a piece of notepaper and squinted at it while I held the flashlight steady.

"Oh, my gosh, I think this is an early draft of a Dylan song."

"Is that good?"

"Yes, but even more so if it's written and signed by Bob Dylan himself. Let's get this stuff down from here."

Scarlet went down first. I handed her the first suitcase, then the second.

"Is there anything else?"

I turned for a final look. And there, almost out of sight, partially obscured by the planks on the floor, was what looked very much like a guitar case. I went over. I was right. I brought it to the opening and lowered it down.

"You're kidding," Scarlet said. "I can't believe this."

We carried everything down to the living room. Scarlet moved the laptop and the library books and cleared the large coffee table. I laid the case in the center.

"You ready?"

"You open it. I'm too nervous."

I unlatched the case and opened it. We both stared.

"Is that it?"

"I think so."

She pulled out the picture and compared it.

"Looks like the same guitar."

"It looks a lot less ugly in the photograph."

"You think it's ugly? I don't know, I think it's kind of cool. And actually it does look a little bit like an axe."

Although I've never been a musician, for a while I considered a career as an audio engineer so I spent some time around guitars. I mostly know the two big makers, Fender and Gibson. I've also seen cool guitars made by Gretsch and Guild. That's about all I know.

"Is this what all the fuss was about?"

"I guess so."

"Do you recognize it?"

"No, but I know the name Gibson. They're really famous."

"Oh, sure, even I've heard of them. Jerry Garcia played a few Gibsons, back in the early days. But nothing that looked like this."

Under the case there was a manila envelope. I picked it up and showed it to Scarlet.

"Open it."

I did as she asked, and removed several pieces of paper. A snapshot fell to the floor. Scarlet picked it up.

"I don't believe it."

She turned it around and showed me. It was of an older man wearing a flannel jacket and one of those hunting caps with the flaps on the side. Standing next to him was a boy, holding something in his hands.

"What is that, a gun?"

"It's the guitar. Look closer."

There was writing on the back. It said: "with Grandpa Larry, Kalamazoo, Mich. April 1960."

"That's my dad with his grandpa. He grew up in Michigan. April 1960 means my dad was 13 at the time. What are those papers?"

"Some kind of receipts. It says 'bill of lading' at the top."

"Shipping receipts, for merchandise. My grandfather and great-grandpa were both truckers. In fact, my dad used to joke that the reason he wanted to be a musician so badly was because he didn't want to end up like them, just driving all the time. He told me that as a musician he drove twice as much as they ever did." She laughed. "Isn't that hilarious? Yeah, I think secretly my dad was pretty happy hanging up his velvet suits and frilly shirts and becoming a regular guy on the train to the city every morning, working in an office."

I looked the receipts over more closely.

"It says there was equipment going from the Gibson factory in Kalamazoo, headed for Chicago, a place called NAMM. It's dated July, 1957. The other is a duplicate, and this one looks like a receipt for the return trip."

"Look at the bottom. Something's been crossed out. Can you read it?"

"It's pretty faded, but it looks like it says 'Received payment from D.M. for unused prototype. $75. L. Brennan."

"L. Brennan is my great-grandpa, Larry Brennan. My dad was always so meticulous about keeping records of everything, from tax records to vinyl records and everything in between. Now I know where he got it from. Looks like it ran in the family."

"It was smart of him to keep it, in case anyone later accused him of stealing it. But who's D.M.?"

"I have no idea."

"Who'd want such an ugly guitar anyway?"

"You think it's ugly? I think it's really cool."

"Why would anybody be so desperate to steal it that they'd kill for it? Assuming Pete was telling the truth, that is. He didn't strike me as the most reliable source."

"It could be worth a lot of money."

"I've seen guitars on Antiques Roadshow go for ten, twenty grand."

"That's enough to kill for, don't you think? I doubt Pete would make something like that up. Especially when everybody already knew about the Far Out. What he said about Gavin worries me, though. It's just crazy enough to be true."

"You said Gavin is—was—a friend. Do you think he'd really conspire against you like that?"

"The Gavin I knew and loved wouldn't, no. But how well did I really know him? Like I said, the scene in Maine had changed for the worse. Instead of being a hippie paradise it was starting to look more like a Stephen King novel. Maybe Gav was taking too much

Far Out, and it messed his brain up like it messed up Pete."

"So why would Martin get involved?"

"His number was on the picture, because I had written it down when I talked to him. Gavin must have called him to find out about the guitar, and then Pete called, not wanting to be cut out of any deal."

"You said Martin was very persistent. I saw it myself, twice. The first time he seemed scared and he said he needed to speak with you, that it was important. The second time he tried running me over. He was aggressive. That doesn't make sense to me. Why would he run away scared, then try running me down?"

"I don't know. Maybe he thought you'd try to hurt him. Maybe the first time was fear, and the second time was self-defense."

"Why? I never saw the guy before."

"Did you hear what Pete said, in the store? He made it seem like there was someone else involved."

"He also said that the kitty-cat had come back for his flower."

"Good point. So you think it was just the drugs talking?"

"Most likely." She looked at the guitar. "One thing's for sure, I want to find out what this guitar is worth, so I at least know for my own peace of mind. Do you know a place I could bring it? Maybe Sam Ash?"

"You could, but I also know a place in Brooklyn if you feel like taking a ride out there."

"I'd like that. Tomorrow? I'm so beat I feel like I could sleep for two days."

"You think it's safe here?"

"I think so. Pete's on the run from the cops, he's not going to come here. Especially since he forgot his cap gun at the store." She snickered. "I shouldn't laugh, the guy is so messed up and I'm partly to blame for his problems. I'll be fine."

"What about the guitar? If that's what everyone wants, who knows who else might be desperate enough to try something?"

"This is my house. I'm not going to live in fear."

The way she said it I could see real inner strength behind that hippie smile. I was going to suggest taking the guitar to my place, but that wasn't exactly a secure environment either.

"All right then, have a good night. We can head out there any time you want."

"Cool. Oh, and I wanted to tell you something, Bert Shambles."

"What?"

"Crashing at your place the other night. It was really nice. We should do it again sometime."

"I'm sure China would love that," I laughed.

Scarlet kissed me on the cheek. "I hope you won't be offended if I say this, because you're so much younger, but there's a quality in you that reminds me of my dad. I think that's why I feel so comfortable around you, so good. It's nothing weird, just a nice feeling."

"Where I come from, feeling nice is pretty weird."

"You poor boy. Call me tomorrow."

CHAPTER 22: G STRING

The next day I was heading out to pick up Scarlet when Aku stopped me in the hallway.

"I have that finger flasher for you, plus some flash paper for you to practice with."

I thanked him and put the paper in my wallet, so it wouldn't get sweaty, and the flasher in my front pocket. I had to admit, it did a pretty good job of frightening the nerds at the 4-D party, but I was pretty sure they were only goblins. I'd have to see how it worked against a troll.

Williamsburg was hopping. Scarlet had her head out the window, taking it all in.

"Oh, man, this is great! I've only hung out in Williamsburg a couple of times. I forget sometimes how close the city is, but how much of a totally different world it is. I can just feel the energy and creativity around me."

She was happier than I'd seen her. We were close enough to the music store that I started looking for a place to park the hatchback.

Scarlet took a deep breath, eyes closed. Then she pulled her head back into the car, spun toward me and opened her eyes.

"Have you noticed how many people are wearing golf outfits?"

"I think it's the hot new style," I said.

"I'm really out of step with the times."

"Me too."

Scarlet paused and gave me a squint, like she was trying to figure me out.

"That's what I don't get. If I could do it all over again I'd totally look for a place like this to live. It's vibrant, exciting, and there are young people everywhere. Wouldn't you rather be in a place like this, instead of stuck way out on the Island with nothing to do?"

"I got into a bit of trouble. I'm on probation for a few years before my record is cleared."

"I don't remember learning that about you from the news."

"Most places were kind about it, since it had nothing to do with what happened over the summer. Kind of conflicts with your idea of me as a hometown hero, doesn't it?"

"Not at all," she said. "A hero without flaws isn't a hero at all; he's a saint. It's overcoming the flaws that makes someone a hero."

"And finding a good parking spot," I added. "Here's one."

I maneuvered the hatchback into the parking space, around the corner from Metropolitan. I went to the back, got the guitar, and joined her on the sidewalk.

"It's around the corner."

I heard about The G String from my friend Cassie, who runs Cassie's Closet. She buys the vintage clothes I sometimes find at the thrift shop. Once I bought an old tube amp at the store for thirty dollars, and Cassie told me to bring it to her friend Dave, that he'd be fair with the price. It was an old Ampeg amp in great condition. Dave put it up for three-fifty and it sold in a day. I earned two-fifty from the sale. Scores like that don't happen very often. I was hoping we'd get lucky again with the guitar.

Dave is a mellow guy with scruffy, dirty blond hair, a strong build, and a very calm, easygoing manner. He's the kind of guy I'd probably hang around with if I lived in Williamsburg. Scarlet gawked at the guitars hanging on the walls in two rows on either side of the narrow, crowded shop. Dave smiled and reached out his hand.

"Hey, man, I remember you. Ampeg Reverberocket, right?"

"That was me."

"Did I see you on the news a few weeks back? Some crazy thing with a golf guy?"

"That was me."

"Cool, I thought so. Man, I think I priced that amp too low. Could've probably got five bills for it, in retrospect. Sorry about that."

"No problem. Hopefully we can make it up with this."

I put the case on the glass counter and spun it around. Dave unlatched and opened the case. He whistled.

"Nice. Moderne reissue. Don't tell me you found this at a thrift shop?"

"It was my dad's," said Scarlet. "He was a rocker, way back." She was grinning ear to ear. I could tell that she was in her element, she loved the whole scene.

"What can you tell us about it?"

"Not much without looking it up, but basically it's a reissue of a guitar that doesn't exist. Back in the 1950s Gibson supposedly made some prototypes of this guitar, but nobody has ever seen one, there are no photographs of them. It's like the Bigfoot of guitars. Anyway, the legend around this mythical guitar got so big that Gibson decided to make a limited edition, based on the original specs. Those are now quite valuable. I'd say this is probably worth four, five thousand dollars. Except..."

Dave spun the guitar around expertly in his hands a few times. He examined different areas of the guitar. He frowned.

"That's strange."

"What?"

"I'd expect there to be a serial number on the back of the headstock, here, as per usual for Gibson. That's where they put their serial numbers. But there's nothing."

"What does that mean?" asked Scarlet. "Is that bad?"

"I don't know. It makes me think that maybe the neck was broken at some point, and a replacement was put on. Maybe the number was filed off at some point. But I usually only see that with forgeries."

"You're saying this is fake?"

"No, not at all." Dave laid the guitar gently back in the case. "I'm just saying that it would take a bit of research. I'd have to take the back plates off and examine the electronics, stuff like that. It's most likely a reissue, though. I'm not trying to bum you guys out."

"I'm just curious," I said. "When were those reissues made?"

"Sometime in the 1980s," he said. Scarlet straightened upright.

"1980s?! Then it can't be a reissue!"

"Why not?"

"What if we told you we have evidence that this guitar is from the 1950s."

Dave snorted. "What, like a real Moderne? No way, man. Not possible."

"I'm just saying 'what if'? If there was such a thing as a real Moderne, what would it be worth?"

"A lot more than a reissue, that's for sure."

"Like ten, fifteen grand?"

"No way."

"More, or less? Do you mean seven, eight grand? Or like twenty?"

"No, I'm talking more like a million dollars or more."

"How much?" Scarlet practically screamed.

"Like a million or more. Who knows, maybe that's too low. Finding an original Moderne would be the Holy Grail of guitars, it might be the most valuable electric guitar ever made." Dave looked us both over.

"Look, I don't want to pry into your business, but if you guys are thinking of passing this off as some kind of original, I would advise against it. The experts would spot it in a minute. I could probably find some flaws in it but it would take me longer. There have been fake ones on the market before, so if your dad bought it thinking it was the real deal, it would depend on what your dad paid for it."

"It wasn't my dad, it was actually his grandpa who bought it for him. I'm not sure but I think he paid seventy-five bucks."

"Wow, that's a great price. It's a really nice copy. I could probably get seven, eight hundred for it without authentication, or like I said, four or five grand if it's a genuine reissue."

Some customers came in. The G String fills up quickly; there's very little free floor space with all the used amps, effect pedals and other paraphernalia crammed in there. I shook Dave's hand and thanked him, and Scarlet gave him a coy wave and took a business card. I picked up the guitar and we excused ourselves past the new customers and went back out into the heat. When we got to the sidewalk she stopped me.

"Hey, why didn't you tell him about the paperwork we found? That and the photo pretty much confirm it. It's totally original, it's got to be."

"I know. But look at what this guitar has already done to people. It's like the ring of power in *Lord of the Rings*. It corrupts people."

"I don't follow. He seems trustworthy."

"Sure, for now. But who else would he tell? How do we know who might find out? No, we need to be very careful about how we proceed with this."

"I could contact one of the major auction houses, like Sotheby's."

"That would be smarter. Maybe make contact online. I could see Dave's brain getting overloaded. He looked right at it, examined it. His mind couldn't accept the fact that it might be real, he dismissed it out of hand."

"It's like that old saying, it's easier to get people to believe a lie than it is to get them to believe they've been lied to."

"Exactly."

"So what do we do now?"

"We find a place to have lunch. Just you, me, and the Precious."

CHAPTER 23: MOM, NATURALLY

We got back to Scarlet's house in the late afternoon. I unloaded the guitar and started up the walk.

"I'd feel better if you held onto it."

"Me? Why?"

"Because I trust you. Also, everyone knows where I live and I've already been broken into once. Pete is somewhere out there and so is Martin."

"I'm worried about you, not the guitar."

"That's sweet. I'll call China and see if she can stay over, or I'll go over to her place. At least you have that groovy wizard to do some ala-kazam on anybody who tries messing with you."

"What if the Precious turns me evil too?"

"It's a chance I'll have to take."

Scarlet gave me a big hug. "Thanks for everything, Bert Shambles. I've had a great day. The past few days have been crazy, but I'm glad I've gotten to know you."

"Same here."

I watched as she swayed into the house. She gave a final wave and closed the door. I heard the deadbolt engage and felt a little better. I laid the guitar case on the back seat of the Olds, then made my way back to Main Street. As I got to the intersection, I saw a Channel 12 news truck. After two suspicious deaths a couple of days apart, Mumfrey was once again the place to be. It made me shudder. My brush with fame earlier in the summer showed me very clearly how destructive fame could be, and how seductive. Maybe it was an instinct triggered by the memory but I decided to see if my mom was home. It was a good night to catch up with her and order in some food. What Aria had said to me about her and my dad was still burning in the back of my mind, like a tire fire at the town dump.

I took the back way, behind the pond and up the back of the hill. Her car was in the driveway. There was just enough room for me to squeeze the Olds next to her blue Chevy. I went around to the other side and took the guitar from the back seat. As I went up the steep stairs the front door opened.

"As I live and breathe. Do I know you, young man? I was beginning to forget what you looked like."

"Hi, mom."

I gave her a kiss and went inside.

"Are you learning how to play the guitar?"

"No, just holding onto this for a friend."

"Speaking of music, I've been watching the story about that musician they found dead. The same group where that young man was electrocuted the other day."

"Do they have any updates about the case?"

"I don't know."

I ran to the living room and put the guitar down next to the couch. My sudden movements disturbed Scram, one of mom's ancient cats, who was snoring sphinx-like on the back of the couch. Scram opened her eyes and wheezed a threatening hiss at me.

The news was on a commercial break. My mom sat on the couch next to me.

"You got your cast off, I see. Does it feel okay?"

"Feels fine."

"You could have called to let me know."

"It's not a big deal. It's a cast, and now it's off. We can order Chinese for dinner if you want."

"The Chinese place down the street closed. It's a bar-b-que place now. Very good. I've got a menu around here someplace."

The news came back on. They led with the story about Pete.

"Shh! I need to see this."

The banner along the bottom of the screen said "Rock & Roll Mystery". The newscaster said that a second member of the band Phowl was found dead, and that police were treating it as a murder investigation and looking more closely at the first tragic death. The leader of a New England biker gang, Larry "Lizard" Cantrell was being held for questioning. The other two members of the band, Tommy Childs and James Overton, had been questioned and released and would be heading back to Maine, where they would prepare a memorial service for their bandmates.

Then the anchor said that they had an exclusive interview with a close friend of the band Phowl, a local woman who went to school with Gavin. They cut to a lady reporter who was standing with Scarlet. My mom started to say something about pulled pork and I shushed her again.

It was a short segment. The reporter asked Scarlet how she knew the band, and what they were like. If Scarlet had been surprised or unhappy about a news truck pulling up to her house and putting her on the news, she didn't show it. She looked completely comfortable in front of the camera.

The reporter asked about Gavin and Brent and made a sad face. Scarlet stayed composed and said that she had loved Phowl since they formed at her college, and that the two victims were great human beings. I could tell by the way the reporter pressed her for her reaction that she wanted Scarlet to cry. I knew from my own experience with the media that news people do creepy stuff like that because it's considered "good television." Scarlet was so sincere and natural that I hoped if I were ever killed that she'd be the one to talk about me. Aria would have probably just given the camera the finger and punched the reporter. Which was also kind of awesome to think about.

The camera panned back to Scarlet for one more question: Had she spoken to police yet? "No," said Scarlet. The lady reporter made a serious face and closed by saying that investigators might want to speak to her about what she knows.

The next short segment was unrelated, but even more interesting. It briefly mentioned that, also in Mumfrey, a man suspected of trying to break into the Rosemary & Time Nostalgia Shop led police on a brief chase before getting away. Anyone with information was asked to call a local crime hotline.

Then it went to a story about a whistling dog. I clicked off the set.

"So Pete got away. Good job, Arnie."

"What are you talking about?"

"Nothing."

"That blonde. Do you you know her?"

"Yes. She hired me to do some work at her place."

"She's quite beautiful. Certainly a lot better than that Mafioso's daughter you've been canoodling around with."

Even though she'd never met her, my mom had decided that she didn't like Aria. It had nothing to do with the mafia, however; I suspected it had more to do with the fact that I was injured during my brief association with Aria, and that my mom's natural instincts were trying to protect her only child by blaming someone else for my problems. Which is what moms do, but still. I decided to set the old lady straight.

"First of all, Scarlet is a lesbian."

"That's all right. You can marry lesbians nowadays."

"Mom, I've already explained it to you. Gay marriage doesn't mean gays get to marry straights. It means they can marry each other. Understand?"

"Of course, I do, I'm not an idiot. I just think someone like that pretty blonde woman would make a better daughter-in-law than that *goombah*."

"Aria was awesome. Please don't insult her."

"What do you mean *was* awesome? Have you two broken up?"

I winced. I sometimes forget that I need to watch my words more carefully around mom.

"Yes. We are no longer dating. Please keep your happy dance to yourself or I'll have my Mafioso friends break your kneecaps."

"That's no way to talk to your mother."

"Oh, yeah?" I leveled my gaze at her. "Know what else isn't nice? Hearing rumors about my dad. That's not very nice either."

"What rumors? What do you mean?"

"I mean that before you talk trash about Aria, maybe you should take a closer look in the mirror."

"You're not making sense."

"Okay, then how's this: there's gossip around town that you were unfaithful to dad, and that's why he left, and that maybe he isn't even my real father."

"Who said that? Who's saying such things?"

"Don't change the subject. A friend of mine met someone who claims he knew both of you back then. He told my friend the rumors."

"What's his name? Do I know this mysterious gossip?"

"Captain Mickey."

"Captain Mickey? There's a name I haven't heard in years. I thought he moved far away, maybe to California. He said that I cheated on your father?"

"He's in California. San Diego. He didn't claim it was true; he said it was one of the rumors that he'd heard."

"San Diego, that's right." My mom looked into the distance. "Didn't you tell me that Mafioso's daughter went to San Diego?"

"Stop changing the subject! Captain Mickey also heard stories that dad might have been in trouble of some kind, and had to leave town."

"I see." She looked away.

"What?"

"I never cheated on your father. Ever."

"So why do people think that you did?"

"It's not something I think I should talk about."

"Mom, you've got to! I believe you, but then I at least have a right to know why people would say something like that, don't you think?"

"Not if it'll hurt you. You're asking me to do the one thing that is unthinkable for a mother, to say or do something that might hurt her own son."

"You have no problem saying the girl I love is a goombah."

"That's different."

"I'm a big boy; I'm sure I can handle it. And I'm not leaving here until you tell me."

She took a sip of wine. "All right. But you have to be patient with me. You stroll in here and suddenly start demanding to talk about things that I haven't spoken to anyone about since your dad was around."

"I'm not going anywhere."

"Fine. Your dad got involved in some things. Dangerous things. He never abandoned us, but he had to leave. We spread that rumor about my infidelity ourselves, as a cover story. We needed a story to make it sound realistic."

"Are you serious? Is dad like in a witness protection program or something?"

"Ha! That's a good one. I wish. Then maybe we all could have been together. Besides, some powerful people were involved and did everything possible to smear your dad and make our lives miserable. Boy, they sure succeeded."

"You're telling me we were in danger? And dad had to leave to protect us?"

"Yes." She sighed. "Except it's been so long now, the time went so fast, that I sometimes wonder if it really happened at all, or if it was some grand delusion we told ourselves to cover the fact that we were having marriage problems."

"Now that you're talking about it, looking back on it, what does your gut tell you? Was the danger real or imagined?"

"Real," she said. "Very real. And very, very frightening."

"What was it?"

"I can't go into it all, at least not yet. I've spent so much time and energy making myself forget everything. I can't just snap my fingers and make it all come back instantly. Give me time. These are painful memories."

"If we were in danger, why didn't we go with him?"

"And do what, live on a sailboat for the rest of our lives? It might sound glamorous but believe me, it's not. It was no way to raise a child. I thought we should stay together and at least give it a shot, but your dad was adamant that it was too dangerous. He's the one who set me up with my job, working for Vinnie Barbarino. He had enough information to believe that we'd be all right, as long as he was gone. So we concocted that cover story and he let the word out at the club—discreetly, of course, which guaranteed that it would be gossiped about endlessly. So he left and I cut ties to the club, which I loved so much, and even my parents turned against me for a while. It's never been the same with them since, because I just couldn't say anything at first, and then after time went by and the wounds healed, I thought that bringing them up again would just open up a bunch of pain, and possibly danger for us."

"Heck of a cover story. You couldn't have come up with anything better?"

"It had to sound plausible, or at least realistic. Everyone was having affairs, sleeping around. It wasn't a big deal. There was endless speculation about who it might be with, and, of course, all the wives got nervous and jealous and kept their husbands away from me, so I lost almost all the friends I'd made at the club. A few true blue women stood by me and didn't judge, or at least knew the hypocrisy of the other women, but the rest—good riddance."

"So he claimed he was heartbroken, and that he doubted I was even his child. I helped him pack; I helped him make the plan. I helped him get away." She was crying now. "It will be hard for you to understand, but it was an act of love, his leaving, and it was a terrible choice we had to make."

"Why didn't you get help, or find someone to trust, or go to the police?"

My mom rolled her eyes. "Ha! It went right up into the local government, the police, everybody. Not that every individual was corrupt, but every institution at that time was tainted. Your dad found out some of what was going on and suddenly things started happening to him. Traffic tickets, flat tires, broken windows, threatening calls, business and tax audits, fines for everything and anything. It was coordinated harassment."

"And you can't tell me what it's about?"

"No. And honestly I don't know much. Certainly not enough to prove anything. Your dad wouldn't tell me anything, for fear it would make me a target too. What was the term he used? 'Plausible deniability,' that was it."

"And you never thought to tell me any of this before? Even a hint, something?"

"I wanted to! You have no idea how difficult it's been. I was waiting for you to be a legal adult, until you turned 21. That way you'd be able to make your own decisions about how to handle the information, and I wouldn't feel pressured to make a choice that might hurt us both. I'd hoped you'd finish college and get a job and be more independent, but then you dropped out and got into all that trouble with the trial. I've only just gotten used to having you back here and I didn't want to tell you something that would send you off on some fool's errand, trying to track down your father."

"Why did you think I'd do that?"

"Oh, please. You're barely out of trouble and in your own place and the first thing you do is go off and track down a killer, nearly get yourself killed in the process. Tonight you come in with a guitar, and there's a man who's been killing musicians on the news, and you happen to know a woman who's involved. The apple didn't fall far from the tree."

"But at the very least I can tell everybody the truth about you, so people don't think you're some kind of hussy."

"No! Bert, listen to me. I need you to promise that you will never tell anyone what I've told you. Nothing, none of it." I wanted to argue with her about it but the look of pure fear on my mom's face frightened me. I nodded.

"Okay. For now."

"Good. And while you're living back in town and waiting for your own legal issues to be resolved, I'd appreciate it if you didn't keep getting involved in these other problems."

"I'm not exactly looking for trouble."

She cocked an eye at me. "Are you sure about that?"

I sat in stunned silence for a minute. I couldn't wrap my mind around what my mom had told me, which in itself isn't particularly surprising. Sometimes I feel like I couldn't wrap my mind around a hot dog if my life depended on in. I'm not talking about one of those big ones, either. I mean one of those little cocktail weenies.

Mom picked up the menu from the coffee table and started scanning it.

"Do you want to eat there or have it delivered?"

I stood up from the couch.

"Can I take a rain check?"

"I thought you said you weren't going anywhere."

"There's something I have to do. I'll be back soon."

Mom sighed. "That's what your dad said."

CHAPTER 24: TELLING THE GODFATHER NO

I said good-bye to my mom and left in a kind of daze, guitar in hand. Instinct told me to bring the guitar in case Martin or someone else had followed me to my mom's house, but otherwise I was on autopilot. Everything looked different. It was like I was on a mega-dose of Far Out, or Farther Out, except much better. The early evening sparkled around me, the air exploded with the sounds of birds and cicadas, the air was like warm honey in my nostrils. The world was brand new.

If he left to protect us, my whole world was more upside down than I'd imagined possible, but for once it was a good feeling. Certain truths I'd taken for granted instantly evaporated. All the guilt and shame I'd felt, that my birth had somehow driven him away: poof. The anger that he'd been too selfish and lazy to live up to his responsibilities: poof. The thought that he didn't care about us? Poof.

Was she being paranoid? Possibly. Moms have that tendency, I've noticed. Or maybe it was how she dealt with the guilt she felt, by concocting this story that grew more and more elaborate over the years. No, that didn't sound right. Mom might exaggerate a bit, especially if she's had a few drinks, but she wasn't crazy or a liar.

Whatever danger or dark feeling her words carried, like a storm on the horizon that could blow open any minute, I also felt a sense that something was being swept out of me. Rows of dominoes stretching way back into my past started toppling over; it was like I'd been given the key to the mysterious, unbreakable code that had defined my life until then, the central question that had always dogged me: why had my dad abandoned me?

I got in the Olds and started driving. I had no destination; I just needed some fresh air and time to think. I thought about Aria, and how she'd tried to help, and how I treated her. I wouldn't have had the conversation with my mom if she hadn't made the effort to find out about my dad and then tell me. I was so blinded by my own pain and feelings of rejection that I'd denied any possibility that there could be a different explanation, and then lashed out at her. Aria had only passed along what my parents had wanted people to believe. And she'd flown across country on a moment's notice to deliver the information, because she understood how important it was to me, even if I didn't.

She understood.

I grabbed my phone to call her, then stopped. Mr. Barbarino had told me not to contact her. I could text her and explain, but I'd given my word. I had no intention of being underhanded or deceptive, especially not with a guy like Mr. Tortura. There was only one way to handle it. I laughed and let the Olds do the rest.

The light, airy feeling stayed with me as I rumbled down the street. The wind blew my hair, I waved to random people, none of whom waved back. The same thought kept looping through my head: I have a dad. I have a dad. He loves me. He loves me.

At the corner of Shore Road I realized my destination. I turned the car this way and that but I was in no rush. I took Shore Road down to the end, when it turned into Yellers Point Road. I kept going up Yellers Point and gave the Olds gas. The 442 bubbled under my command like a thoroughbred.

Driving into Pondington really feels like entering a different world. It's the rich section of Mumfrey, and is pretty nice as far as rich neighborhoods go. It's an old area, filled with even older money. Most of the larger, older homes aren't even visible from the street. Just gates with high-tech security equipment, set every few hundred feet in the woods. The Torturas made no effort to hide their wealth; in fact, they went overboard trying to broadcast their money and power to all who passed. With its columns, lights, and bright colors, the compound is hard to miss. One rumor I heard was that they kept the place so bright to make it harder for Sicilian assassins to sneak onto the property. The front gate was open so I pulled up to the circle in front of the house, in front of a marble statue that was spitting water at me. The next thing I knew I was standing at the front door, ringing the doorbell.

The door swung open. I recognized the guy standing there as one of Aria's many, large, and mean brothers. The last time I'd seen this one he was hanging out of the side of a Cadillac, searching the town so they could beat me to a pulp. I don't know what kind of reception I was expecting, but I'd hoped that the fact that I saved his sister's life might have softened his opinion of me somewhat. I was wrong. His expression made it clear that I wouldn't be getting a Facebook friend request from him anytime soon. Which was fine with me, because I wasn't on Facebook anyway.

"What do you want? Aria ain't here. Get lost."

He was about to slam the door in my face when I heard a voice behind him.

"Frank? Who is it? Is it someone for me?"

The human mountain otherwise known as Frank rolled his eyes and stepped to the side. Aria looked happy to see me.

"Bert! What are you doing here?"

"Aria, you know you ain't supposed to see this clown no more."

"Shut up, Frank. Get out of here. I'll handle this."

The big thug snorted and went off. I heard a door slam.

"What brings you here? What is it?"

"Good evening, Miss Tortura. Is your father home?"

"My dad? Yes, he's in his office. Why?"

"I need to speak with him. Please take me to him."

Aria must have sensed that I was in a zone and not to be trifled with, because she didn't say another word; she bowed her head slightly and led me across the large marble foyer, through a set of gilded white doors and down a dimly-lit carpeted corridor, to another set of large wooden doors that were more plain and natural looking, stained with a clear varnish and with huge gold-plated knobs. She knocked gently and a voice told her to enter. She pushed open the door and leaned her head in.

"You have a visitor."

"Who is it?"

She stepped back and motioned for me to enter.

I went into the office. There was a giant desk at one end, surrounded by impossibly ornate furnishings. Beyond it was a huge solarium, with palm trees and fountains. A lemon tree was growing under a huge glass skylight, next to a dark stone wall that housed an enormous fireplace. Mr. Tortura looked up from his work. He had salt-and-pepper hair and a thick mustache, but he didn't look anything like a detective. He looked like a guy who didn't like unexpected visitors and knew how to handle such people without any help.

"Can I help you?"

I walked into the center of the room and stopped.

"We've never met. My name is Bert Shambles."

A large smile spread across his face. He came around the desk and shook my hand, then offered me one of the chairs.

"Bert! We meet at last. Please, sit down."

I sat in one of the chairs. He went back behind the desk and sat down, then swiveled and pointed to a large wooden bookcase against one wall. A TV stood in the center. A show was on. There was a lady with big hair, putting her fingers to her temples.

"Have you ever seen this show, *Long Island Medium*?"

"No, sir."

"This lady is amazing. She can tell people all about their loved ones, their past, their dearly departed. My grandmother had the same ability."

We watched for a few more seconds, then he pressed a button on the remote and screen went dark. He swiveled back to face me.

"What's on your mind, young man? I understand Mr. Barbarino paid you a visit."

"Yes. Thank you for that, I greatly appreciate it."

"Of course. It was the least I could do, considering your kind actions on behalf of Aria."

"That's why I came to speak to you. I wanted to tell you that as much as I appreciate your help, I cannot accept the terms that Mr. Barbarino described."

Mr. Tortura's jawline tightened slightly and something in his eyes changed. It was the same kind of expression, I noticed, that comes over Aria just before she slaps me. In that instant I could see that he would be a horrifying man to cross.

"Oh? I hope you did not think the offer was negotiable, because it wasn't."

"No, I don't think it's negotiable. Because it's not a deal at all. You claim it was a way to thank me for helping Aria, but really it was a demand, using my actions as a justification. You bought me a few hours of freedom, and I am truly grateful for that, but in exchange you're asking for my life."

"What do you mean?"

"You're forcing me to give up the woman I love. That's a worse sentence than anything the police might have tried giving me, especially since I can prove my innocence."

Mr. Tortura stood up and placed his fingertips on the desk in front of him. His complexion was slightly more pink, but he was clearly trying to contain his temper.

"So you came here to disrespect me here, in my home, and tell me that you're defying my wishes despite my efforts to help you?"

"I'm telling you that you can't repay a debt with a demand and a threat. That's not a repayment at all. What you've given me is meaningless compared to what you're taking. I came here out of respect, to tell you man to man, because I do not believe in deception. I care very deeply about Aria, and respectfully ask your permission to date her, if that's what she wants. But I won't be bullied or roll over for anyone, no matter how powerful he is."

"Stop!"

We both turned toward the door, startled. Aria stood there, hands balled into fists at her side. Tears were streaming down her face. Our eyes locked, and she ran across the carpet and took a leap into my arms. She wrapped her arms around my head and kissed me on the lips, cheeks, eyes and nose, over and over again.

"You said you loved me."

"I said...I care...deeply...about you," I said between kisses.

"Before that," she purred. "You said you couldn't be away from the woman you loved. Oh, sweetheart." Kiss kiss etc. etc. kiss kiss etc.

Aria slid weightlessly out of my arms, wiped her face with her hands and turned to her father.

"Daddy, if you say or do anything to break us up I swear you will never see me again."

"But, Aria—"

"No! Listen to me, Daddy. If you send my boyfriend away, I swear I'll move away from here and cut off all contact. I'll get a job in a strip club and dance for tips. I don't care. I'll never touch a dime of your money or have anything to do with this rotten family ever again."

Mr. Tortura paused before speaking again. Like any shrewd businessman, even one who had probably killed people, he appeared to be weighing the sincerity of his opponents—one of whom happened to be his baby girl. Finally, he broke his gaze and shrugged.

"It was never my intention to drive you two apart. I only wanted to be sure of the young man's character." Then he looked at me, but it wasn't threatening like before. "Young man, you live in a manner I do not understand or approve of, in that old house that's falling down. I don't mind if you're not rich, because I was poor when I was a young man, but I'm concerned that you have no ambition. You work for the church, I respect that, but you have no education, no career, and you appear to have a lot of trouble with the law."

"Quit while you're ahead, Papa."

He laughed sadly. "Okay, I won't say any more. It's perfectly reasonable for a father to want his children to marry well. Not just financially, but someone with an eye to the future, who cares about family and career and has ambition. But, eh, what do I know? I only want you to be happy, my daughter. If this young man makes you happy, and if he's enough to keep you here for a while and stay close to your family, I cannot refuse that."

"That's not enough," Aria said. "You have to tell the boys not to give him a hard time any more, ever, and all

of you need to treat Bert with respect and kindness.
Bert must be welcome in this house any time he wants
or needs to be, or it's a disgrace. I'm not ashamed of
him, I'm ashamed of all of you and how you could treat
a friend like Bert, who's been nothing but wonderful to
me. Okay, he can also be a little weird sometimes, I
admit, but—"

"Quit while you're ahead," I said.

Mr. Tortura nodded.

"I understand. I give you my word that Bert will be
an honored guest in this house for as long as you two
remain friends. Is that what you want me to say?"

"And the boys?"

"They will never again try to hurt him or disrespect
him, unless he hurts you in some way."

"No, under no circumstances. I can take care of
myself."

"It's true," I said. "She can slap really freaking
hard."

I rubbed my cheek for emphasis. Mr. Tortura
grinned broadly.

"I could have told you that."

"Now you two shake on it."

We did as Aria instructed.

"I'm going to leave you two alone," Mr. Tortura
said. He went out of the office and closed the door
behind him. Aria hugged me again and kissed me for
real this time, hard, in that way that makes me lose my
balance and see stars.

"What you did was so brave. No guy I've ever
known had the cojones to talk to my dad like that."

My phone buzzed. I pulled it out.

"Bert, it's Scar. I got a call from China. She knows
someone who can tell us whether the guitar is real or
not. But we have to bring it over there tonight."

"We? Why we?"

"I just figured since you're going to get fifteen percent that you'd like to be involved. So if we cleared even five hundred thousand from the sale of this, your take would be, oh, about seventy-five grand or so."

"I'll be right over."

"Who was that? Is that my competition?"

"No, it's your mother's competition. But she has a guitar that might be very valuable, and she asked me to hold onto it. There's someone who can appraise it for us but I have to go there tonight; he's leaving in the morning."

"How valuable are we talking about?"

"If the guitar is genuine and the initial estimate is correct, I could get a hundred grand out of the deal."

Aria squealed. "A hundred thousand dollars?"

"Maybe more. Maybe a lot more. It all depends."

"What are we waiting for? Let's go!"

"Who, we?"

"Of course." Aria smiled a sly grin and slid her hand into mine. "You don't think I'm letting you out of my sight again, do you?"

CHAPTER 25: CAT FIGHT

We roared out of the Tortura driveway. The Olds 442 loved moments like these; so did its owner. I don't know anything about cars but I know it's a serious classic, worth many thousands of dollars. I take care of it the best I can.

"So you haven't told me what this is all about. Why are you running off to see this woman whose back you tried fixing by—what was it?—oh yes, grabbing her boobs."

"You don't have to come along, you know."

"That's what you think. I want to meet this airhead."

"Stop it."

"Why? Feeling protective of her?"

"No, you."

"I'm not afraid of her."

"Not from her, from yourself. You shouldn't call people names like that. You might go overboard some day and call your boyfriend's mom a 'ho'."

"Good point." Aria looked around the interior. "I've never been in your car before. It's amazing. Where'd you get it?"

"I bought it off a little old lady who only drove it to the supermarket."

"Did you have to squeeze her melons too? "

"Ha ha. But just so you know, you were right."

"Don't tell me you felt up an old lady to get this car!"

"No! My mom. I mean, what you said about her. I got some more information. There's no doubt he's my dad. She didn't sleep around like people said, but she explained why the rumors got started."

"I'm really sorry about that. Your mom must hate me."

"I'm sure she'll like you when she meets you. If you can keep your big mouth shut."

"Good luck with that. Speaking of parents, what were you and my dad talking about? Did he get you out of trouble or something?"

"Mr. Barbarino came by the police station and picked me up. He passed along your dad's wishes that I never see you again."

"Why were you at the police station?"

"It was nothing. They kind of thought I might have killed a guy. It was all a misunderstanding."

"One of my brothers was accused of that. Cops are so crazy."

"Don't I know it."

"So you came over to stand up to my father? That takes major courage, boyfriend. I know he really respects that. But I wouldn't recommend pushing your luck with him."

"I had no intention of doing so."

She turned and looked in the back seat.

"So this guitar is really special?"

"Only if it's authentic and not a fake. Scarlet's friend knows a guy who can tell us. But he's leaving town tomorrow. We have to find out before he goes."

"Ok, so assuming it's real, how much is it worth?"

"We took it to a guy I know in Brooklyn. He said it might be worth a million dollars, maybe more. But he thought it was a fake, or a reissue."

"Hm." She looked out the window, distracted.

"That's right, I forgot. A million dollars is nothing to a girl like you."

"What? No, that's not it. It's just that you took your other woman to Brooklyn. You've never taken me to Brooklyn."

"Next chance I get, I promise."

"So why do you care what this guitar is worth? It's her guitar."

"She offered me a fifteen percent finder's fee."

"You should have held out for thirty percent."

"That's not my style. Bottom line is, I'm part owner of one of the rarest guitars in the world. A hundred grand is a fortune for a guy like me. It could buy a lot of trips to Brooklyn for us."

"I don't want to go to Brooklyn," she sniffed. "We'll go someplace she hasn't been. Like Ibiza or Morocco."

"What's your problem?"

"I'm very tense. When I get tense I want to hit things."

"Make love not war, baby."

"Fine. I won't beat her face in. But you need to assure me of something. I need you to promise me, absolutely swear that nothing happened between you two."

"I totally swear. 100%, absolutely, God's honest truth. Now will you promise me that you won't hit her?"

"Yes, I promise. But I hope you appreciate how difficult that will be for me."

"I do, believe me."

We pulled up to the house. Scarlet was sitting cross-legged on the front lawn, next to a suitcase. She hopped to her feet, picked up the suitcase and bopped over to the car.

"She's way too perky," Aria said. "What's with the suitcase?"

Scarlet slid into the back seat, next to the guitar.

"I thought I'd bring the other memorabilia we found in the attic," she said. "Maybe this friend of China's can appraise some of that stuff too."

"Scarlet, this is Aria. Aria, Scarlet."

"Oh, hey! Bert told me so much about you! Hey, I'm really sorry about the other morning. I'm sure Bert explained what was really going on. It must have seemed really crazy, though." She stuck her hand out to shake. Aria ignored her and stared out the window. After a moment of awkward silence, she shot me a look.

"What? I said I wouldn't kick her ass; I didn't say I'd kiss it."

I could see the words hurt Scarlet. Her eyes narrowed and a sly smirk spread across her face. I had a feeling she had stronger reserves than I'd given her credit for.

Scarlet reached over and ran her fingers through my hair, and spoke in a sultry voice.

"I don't need you to kiss me, honey. Not when your man is such an amazing kisser. Isn't that right, Bert?" She leaned over and nuzzled my right ear. Aria spun around and glared at her.

"What are you talking about? Nothing happened between you two."

"Oops. I'm sorry, Bert. Should I have kept it a secret? The way you grabbed and kissed me behind the pizzeria the other night?"

"Oh, yeah," I said. "I forgot to tell you. We kind of accidentally made out."

"What?!"

"It was only because the bikers were after us!"

Aria turned a new shade of red, then exhaled.

"I know you're trying to rile me up, but it's not going to work. Bert's already told me that you're a lesbian."

"What?! I'm not a lesbian. Why did you tell her that?"

Both women stared at me.

"That's what you said! The whole *Yoga With Lesbians* thing, remember?"

"Oh, that. No, that's China's thing, not mine. I mean, I help her because she's my friend, but I'm straight. I thought I told you that." She clucked her tongue. "No, I didn't. That was right when Brent—the person pretending to be Brent, I mean—called. That explains it. I wondered why you didn't make a move on me; I thought you must not like me because I was making it pretty obvious that I was into you. Oh well, too bad."

"Yeah, I'm real broken up over it," Aria said.

"I bet we'd have had fun together. We could have gone camping upstate. I have an awesome tent."

"I knew it," I groaned.

Aria muttered something in a foreign language. I didn't have to be fluent in Italian to understand what she was saying. "Just wait until I get you alone," she finished in English.

Scarlet reclined in the seat. I could see in the rearview mirror that she was trying not to laugh at it all. I couldn't blame her for being a bit catty, considering how rude Aria had been to her. On the other hand, I also knew enough about women to know that if I said the wrong thing, the two of them would end up fast friends and I'd be the one left out in the cold. I kept my mouth shut and kept driving.

Fiddler's Isle is a strange part of Mumfrey that has kind of been forgotten. It was a commercial fishing village that became home to a collection of small factories during the Second World War. Neither industry was still there, but neither had fully left, either. The area was a hodge-podge of abandoned, broken down old brick industrial buildings and small fishing cottages that now housed what remained of Mumfrey's dwindling working classes. When I was in high school there were certain spots around town that kids might go to on a weekend night, to build a bonfire and maybe smuggle in a keg for an impromptu party. There were parties on golf courses, hidden beaches and in nature preserves where me and my friends would go to feel a bit free and wild and maybe kiss a girl or two if we were lucky. Fiddler's Isle was a perfect location for those kinds of parties, but nobody I knew ever went there or took advantage of it, because it was simply too scary.

I'd wondered why there wasn't massive development there, considering how valuable waterfront property is. My mom told me there were rumors that the ground under the whole area was saturated with heavy metals and toxic chemicals, and that breast cancer rates in that area were several times higher than the rates on the rest of Long Island, which were already supposedly much higher than the national average. I never knew how much faith to put into those old wives' tales and rumors, but there was no denying the fact that the area seemed to have a kind of curse over it. In school I'd heard that the old buildings and rocky shoreline were littered with syringes, that there were unexploded mines still buried there, and that the only people who dared explore out there were druggies and homicidal maniacs.

We turned off Shore Road and went over the nondescript blacktop bridge that crossed the tiny canal that separated Fiddler's Isle from the rest of Mumfrey. There was still a deep blue glow in the sky, but as soon as we crossed the canal, the trees seemed to blot everything out. I put the headlights on high. The interior of the Olds was dark except for the glow from Scarlet's phone as she consulted the map for directions.

"Right on Melville, then four blocks down. Neversink is the last street. Make a left and go to the end."

I did as she instructed. The area was as desolate and frightening as the stories made it out to be. Here and there a small cottage glowed with the lights of a TV. I saw a black dog chained to a pole in a yard. It barked as we rolled by.

I turned left on Neversink and went down to the end. There was a lone cottage there, surrounded by a rubble lot on one side, and a fenced-off area of beach beyond, where it looked like there were once some docks, and now only rusted signs warned *Danger* and *Keep Off* and *Private Property*. From this part of the shoreline, the water looked dark and forbidding, like something to be avoided. I saw a small mailbox, half off its post, next to an overgrown driveway. Number 9.

"This is it."

It was a beaten down cottage, even worse than the rooming-house. One story, set back off the road and obscured by overgrown bushes and lots of random homemade sculptures in the yard, made out of rusting cans, car parts, electrical and plumbing fixtures. A face that used an old faucet and knobs for a nose and eyes.

I got out and took the guitar, then Scarlet got out with the suitcase and looked at the cottage.

"I have this weird feeling I've been here before," she said. "I can't remember when, or why."

There were no lights on anywhere in the cottage. We went up the crumbling front walkway and the screen door creaked open and China came out. She saw me and Aria and frowned.

"What are you doing with him? Who's she?"

"Nice to see you too," Scarlet said. "What is this place?"

"I thought it was only going to be you. They can't be here. They have to go."

"I asked Bert to come. And this is his girlfriend, Aria. We saw her the other day, at Bert's place."

"Oh, yeah, the uptight one. Nice robe."

Aria crossed her arms and growled.

"These guys are cool; they'll just hang out quietly."

"No, they have to go."

"I came with them. And Bert has a right to know about the guitar, since he's going to get a percentage."

"There's not going to be any percentage to get," a man's voice said. It came from inside the cottage. "China, honey, why don't you have your friends come inside?"

"I think you'd better do what he wants," China said.

"Oh, my gosh," Scarlet said. "Now I remember why I was at this house. Your dad used to live here. He made those sculptures in the front yard, with parts from his hardware store. Is that you, Charlie?"

"You have a good memory," the man said. "Lucky for me it was vacant, and the old couple who own it still remembered me. They know how to treat a man with respect. Unlike some people, who don't care if their daddy starves out on the street."

"I want nothing to do you with you," China said.

"Listen." It was Aria. "I don't know who any of you people are, but I'm not setting foot in that rat-trap. Come on, Bert, we're getting out of here."

"You're not going anywhere," the man said. His arm extended from behind the screen door. Attached to the arm was his hand, and attached to that was a very large gun. I don't know anything about firearms but this one definitely did not have 'Roy Rogers' written on the side.

"Like I said, all of you step inside. Now."

CHAPTER 26: HIPPIE HOUSE OF HORRORS

The inside of the cottage was dark and dingy. For once I didn't feel like the biggest slob in the world, just one of the biggest. The layout was what the realtors would call an open floor plan, but for all I knew the builders might have been too lazy to put up walls. There was a ratty, low couch next to a lamp on the floor with a broken shade, bleeding ugly light on the old newspapers that were turning yellow from age, taped over the windows. There were overflowing ashtrays, empty food containers, and the smell of stale, unhealthy air. There was an open kitchen area with an L-shaped counter. The counter tops were crammed with various pieces of what looked like lab equipment; plastic jugs lined the floor.

Charlie was standing off to one side, in the shadows. He had a small build and short graying hair that was almost completely white. He had a rough, unshaven face that looked like it had been on the losing end of a few fights. If he'd ever looked like a budding rock star—and the photo China showed me looked that way—then whatever star quality he once had was long gone. Charlie looked like what he was: a hardened, unforgiving criminal. I know I said I wanted to ask him whether he preferred prison or Long Island, but one look at him answered the question permanently in my mind.

"What's in that suitcase?"

"More stuff of my dad's," Scarlet said.

"Open it up."

She did as he said. She opened the suitcase and spun it around to face Charlie. He glanced down and started laughing.

"Well, ain't that sweet of you, Scarlet. I just wanted a guitar and you're throwing in a free archive of priceless artifacts. You're the best. Now put the guitar down over there."

I did as he asked and put it on the floor in the middle of the room.

"Open it and let me see."

I opened the case.

"My word. That's it, all right. A genuine Gibson Moderne. A buddy of mine says he knows a guy who knows Billy Gibbons. Said Billy would pay two point five mil for this guitar."

I saw a shape out of the corner of my eye. I looked over at a ratty chair in the far corner, shrouded in darkness. The shape was slumped over and tied with duct tape. It was Martin Douglas.

"He doesn't look well," I said. "Did you kill him too?"

"He ain't dead, just gave him something to help him sleep. But you will be if you keep asking questions."

"I'm calling the cops," Scarlet said. She pulled her phone out. Charlie pointed the gun at her.

"I'd hate to have to kill you, darling, but I will."

"Believe him," China said. "He'll kill any of us."

Scarlet lowered the phone. Charlie reached out his free hand and took it from her.

"The rest of you give me your phones too. Don't try anything cute."

We did as he said. As I reached into my pocket and took out my phone, I felt something else in there, something metal. It was the finger flasher that Aku had given me. Fat lot of good that was going to do me. I handed over the phone. Charlie squinted at me.

"You look familiar. You been on TV recently?"

"That depends. Have you been abducted by aliens recently?"

"Cute. Keep it up and you'll be abducted by angels."

There was a small corridor running off the side of the kitchen. A door opened at the end of it and Pete came into the room, rubbing his eyes.

"Wow, man, I think I passed out. What's going on?"

"We've got visitors. Take your medicine."

"Oh, yeah, sure man." Pete pulled out the vial, clamped it under his nose and inhaled deeply, then looked at us.

"Hey, you're the guy from the store. You sent the cops chasing after me. I was too quick for them; they couldn't catch me." He put his arms out like he was flying.

"I can't believe you did this." Scarlet was talking to China now. "I thought we were friends, soul mates."

"China had nothing to do with it. She might take after her old man in some ways, but this was my doing. I had to break into my own building just to get some of my supplies out of the basement."

"It's not your building," China snapped. "It's mine. I pay the mortgage, I kept it going when you went away. Scar, he tricked me here, said he was going to make a deal with me and go away for good. Said I'd never have to see him or talk to him again if I got you to bring over some guitar that he said your dad stole from him. So when you told me about finding a guitar I mentioned it to him."

"I told you not to say anything," I said. Scarlet looked pained.

"I thought I could trust her of all people."

"He told me to get you here with the story about the appraisal. I'm sorry, Scarlet, it really is my fault. I screwed everything up."

"You certainly did," Charlie sneered. "I ask you to do one simple thing, just get my guitar here with Scarlet, alone, and you can't even do that right. She showed up with a whole entourage. Makes things very messy for me, very complicated."

China was crying now. "Just let us go, stop all this."

"It's not your guitar anyway," Scarlet said. "It was my dad's."

"You think so? Who do you think bought that guitar from your grandfather? Your dad didn't want to play guitar, until he found out I was getting that rare beauty. He made his dad give it to him instead, and I got a different guitar. A Les Paul, also very fine and valuable. Wish I still had it. It was a running joke when we were in the band, I used to tell him to take good care of my guitar. I knew that Moderne was worth a fortune, and he did too. One time back in the 80s when I had a little bit of money I offered to buy it from him for a hundred grand. He claimed the guitar had been stolen years ago, but I knew that was a lie. He was too organized and obsessive about holding onto things. So I bought a building instead and started my business, but I went down the wrong road and got myself into trouble. That guitar is going to set me up for life, and nobody's going to get in my way again."

"What was your dad's name?" I asked him.

"Don. Donald Mancuso."

I looked at Scarlet. "D.M.," I said.

"What, you know something about that you're not telling me?" He raised the gun again. "Tell me what you know."

"There was a receipt," Scarlet said. "In the case. It said there was money received from a D.M., seventy-five dollars. But it was crossed out."

"That's because your daddy decided to follow in my footsteps and become a musician too. We were friends at the time, or at least I thought we were, so I didn't mind so much. But over the years he made all that money by selling out, ignoring rock and roll and doing advertisements while I struggled. It got under my skin."

"I never knew any of this," Scarlet said. "I didn't know you resented my dad so much, I never even knew about the guitar until recently."

"And you wouldn't have known anything, if not for Gavin."

"How was he involved?"

"Me and Lizard go way back. He used to move a lot of product for me back in my dealing days. We all hung out in the rock scene, a lot of paths were always crossing. When I got out of the pen, I looked him up, to see if there was any work around, so I could make a buck. He mentioned that your friend Gavin had talked about some rare guitar you had, and how Gavin was scheming to get it from you without you knowing its true value."

"So you killed him to take it for yourself."

"Just a simple accident. He needed to be sent a message not to double-cross anyone else, because he had that habit. Just ask Pete. I swear, for all these musicians sing about love and peace they're really some of the lowest scum you'll ever meet."

"You should know," I said.

"Don't try blaming other people for what you did," China said. "You're holding us all against our will, there's no way you can get away with any of this."

"Sure there is. Because Scarlet here is going to sell me the guitar right now, for what my daddy paid. Seventy-five dollars. Nobody's going to pin anything on me."

"You forgot about Brent. And Martin here might want to talk to the police about kidnapping."

"Nobody's going to tell the cops anything. Pete killed Brent, not me. And Martin's not going to lose his share of the profits on the guitar just to complain about a little party that got a bit too wild." Charlie smiled. "It won't matter once we get this equipment to a safe place and start our new business. Little Pete here is a genius. He's going to be making too much money selling Farther Out to care."

"That's right," Pete sang. "Money, money, and everyone will be happy."

"He can barely tie his shoelaces at this point," I said. "I think it's more likely that you're setting him up to take the fall. What do you think, Pete, that make sense to you?"

"Money money," he giggled. "Happy happy."

"Forget tying his shoes. He couldn't find his ass with a handful of fish hooks and a search warrant," China said. "He's the perfect stooge."

"So you called me, pretending to be Brent?"

"That was Pete's idea."

"'Hey, Scarlet, it's Brent'," Pete mimicked. I had only met Brent once but it sounded like a perfect imitation. Then again, all those hipster-stoner types kind of sound alike, with the same raspy, drawn-out, over sincere kind of drawl. "'The phones are tapped'," he continued, giggling.

"At the Knights of Columbus hall," Scarlet said to Charlie. "In the corridor. That was you."

"No law against a guy dressing up in costume," Charlie said. "Too bad we were interrupted. I was looking forward to getting a piece before I killed you. I always liked you, Scarlet."

Scarlet grunted in disgust.

"Do you hear him?" I said to Pete. "He's setting you up. Don't you care?"

"No way, man, Charlie's a cool dude. He wouldn't do that to me."

"What about Lizard?" I asked. "He's under pressure from what happened to Gavin. How can you be sure of his silence?"

"He won't say anything. Besides, he's getting half the money from the guitar."

"I told you you should have negotiated better," Aria said to me.

"Guitar? What about my cut?" asked Pete. His eyes were wide and wandering all over the room, like they were trying to follow invisible little fairies flying around.

"Don't you get it?" I said. "You're being cheated. Cut out." I reached into my back pocket and took out Pete's iPhone and handed it to him. "Here, give Lizard a call if you don't believe me."

"I told you to give me your phones!" Charlie yelled.

"Yes," I said. "But you didn't tell me to give you Pete's phone."

Pete took the iPhone. "Dude! You are so totally cool. You're the only person not trying to screw me over. I'll call Lizard. He'll know what to do."

"Put that phone down!"

"You're not splitting anything with Lizard," Scarlet said. "You're trying to cut him out too, aren't you? You're lying to everyone."

Pete poked and flicked the screen.

"I said put the damn phone down." Charlie raised the gun. Pete looked up, the glow from the screen illuminating his crazy eyes, as his mouth turned up in a child-like grin.

"Don't make me kill you," Charlie growled. "I need you to take the fall for the rest of these dead bodies."

"You don't control me, man."

Control. Con-trol.

Troll.

I stuffed my hands into my pockets. I slipped the finger flasher onto the finger of my right hand. In my left hand I grabbed a few sheets of the flash paper and crumpled them into a ball.

"I said stop it!"

Pete ignored him. The gun barked and Pete recoiled. He grabbed a shoulder and when he pulled his hand away it was covered it blood. It seemed to stun him back into a moment of clarity.

"You shot me? You freaking shot me?"

I took a step toward Charlie. "Do you believe in magic?"

"Do I what?"

"You heard me. Magic. Do you believe in it?"

"I believe you're going to wind up dead like the rest if you don't shut up."

I closed my eyes and mumbled a spell. It was just gibberish, but I tried to make it look convincing, the way Aku did.

Panka, danka,
ibble-dee-do
Let me do some
magic for you!

I waved my hands around. Charlie looked amused. I flew my hands out and ignited the paper and a giant fire ball flashed in the air between us.

This time it was Charlie who screamed. He took a step back and tripped over the jugs that were against the kitchen counter. Just as he was going down, a giant ball collided with him and knocked him over.

It was Martin Douglas. He was still tied with the duct tape. He had rammed Charlie with a head butt.

Charlie hit the ground hard with Martin on top of him. One of the jugs ruptured and started spilling liquid on the floor. It smelled strong, almost like fingernail polish remover. The gun discharged and clanged off one of the pieces of lab equipment and sparked. Something on the counter started smoking and caught fire. Martin was pinning Charlie down with his weight. Charlie struggled frantically to get free.

"You stupid idiot, do you know what this stuff is? It's going to blow us all to hell! Get off me!"

The fire spread more quickly than I could've imagined. It covered the counter and was rapidly moving down to the liquid on the floor. Pete ran over and pulled Martin off with his good arm, then jumped on top of Charlie and started punching him, over and over again.

"Pete, get out of here!"

Martin stumbled over, still clearly disoriented. Scarlet and Aria took him from either side and hustled him out. I started out but turned and saw China. She was in a panic, screaming at her dad and Pete to stop it, that they were going to die. I ran over and grabbed her. She pushed me off and tried going to her dad, just as the liquid ignited and a wall of flame shot up to the ceiling.

"China!"

"Get away! I need to save my dad!"

I didn't know what else to do. I grabbed her around the waist from behind and lifted her off her feet. She struggled for a second but then her body went limp. The smoke and flames were unbearable. The lids of the jugs were popping, there were terrible hissing and melting noises. I heard the gun fire again and again, a scream, then another scream.

I dragged China out and had her halfway across the front lawn when the first blast happened. A shock wave went through me like the atmosphere itself had kicked me from behind. I lost my balance and was thrown forward. China slipped from my arms and tumbled to the grass. I threw myself over her body as the second explosion blew the cottage to bits. It was followed by a series of explosions, one after the other, as the jugs of chemicals blew. Debris showered around us, a rain of fire and glass, wood and nails, roofing panels and aluminum siding. Then there was just the heat and roar of the fire.

Aria and Scarlet ran over to us. "Are you all right?!"

"I think so."

We all stared at the cottage. It was an inferno.

"Did anyone grab the guitar?" I asked. "Or the suitcase?"

Nobody said anything.

"Well, that sucks," Scarlet said.

Martin was out on the street. A few of the nearby residents had come out of their cottages. He was yelling at them to call 911. I saw China struggling to get up.

"Guys, I think we better help China," I said. "She doesn't look too good."

Scarlet ran to her friend's side, trying to revive her. China was semi-conscious but clearly out of it. She was in tears, saying over and over how sorry she was, how much she loved Scarlet and would never hurt her intentionally. Scarlet soothed her and told it was going to be all right. Then she looked up at me.

"Can you help her up? I don't want to risk any more with this back of mine."

I got China into a standing position. Her body slumped down with no resistance. I grabbed her before she could hit the ground and pulled her close to me.

"Give me a hand!" I yelled to Aria. "I'm going to lose my grip!"

Aria came over, then stopped and stared at me. I saw the expression on her face, then followed her eyes to where they were looking. My hands were covering China's breasts.

"You really are unbelievable," she said.

CHAPTER 27: A NEW DOPE

Pete and Charlie were killed in the blast. China was all right. She spent a night in the hospital, was treated for shock and dehydration and was released. I didn't see her, but she told Scarlet to thank me for getting her out of the house, and told me I could have free yoga at her studio for life. Not exactly a gift I planned on using, but you never know.

Martin made the local news, and he soaked up all the attention. He loved it, and promoted his business like crazy. I drove by once and the parking lot was so full that it was holding up traffic on Main Street. I managed to stay off the TV news this time, but the newspaper and online accounts all mentioned me. One of them even used Scarlet's quote, "hometown hero." If this kept up I was going to have to invest in some alien abduction insurance.

Scarlet went up to Maine for a week, to see her old friends and attend a memorial service for Gavin, Pete and Brent. It was going to be a concert, just the way they would have wanted it. A bunch of local bands were going to play Phowl songs and release doves or something. She said that even though Gavin and Pete might have been trying to cheat her, she wasn't going to let that destroy the good times they'd once shared. She said that when she came back she'd call me so we could finally start her dad's inventory and house sale. "In a way, I feel the guitar really was Charlie's," she said in our last conversation before she headed up to Bangor. "At least in a karmic way. It was a terrible way to die, but I think my dad's spirit needed to be released from the past, once and for all."

I admired her ability to forgive, her seemingly genuine kindness toward even those who wronged her, and told her so.

Lizard and the Wheels were told by local law enforcement never to come through Mumfrey again if they knew what was good for them. At least that was how *Newsday* put it. They were cleared of the murders but now the Feds were looking into allegations of drug-running by the gang. They were going to be tied up with investigations for a long time. I was pretty sure there would eventually be criminal charges, but at least they were gone.

A few days later, Aria and I were spooning on my cot, the fan gently cooling the sweat on our bodies.

"Wow."

"Yeah, wow."

"I'd forgotten how amazing it was."

"I never knew that was even possible."

"How many is that now?"

"Four, five? I lost count."

"Me too. Ready for another?"

"Ready if you are, sexy."

I squeezed her tighter. "I could do this all day. Just you, me, and a *Long Island Medium* marathon."

"How did she know about that guy's dead grandmother?"

"Or the dead dog in that lady's past?"

"Incredible."

Aria wiggled. "What's going on back there?"

"I'm getting a signal."

"Don't get too excited, boyfriend. I told you, no funny business."

"I might not be able to see into your past, but can I at least look at your behind?"

"No. Clothes stay on, I told you. I'm not that type of girl."

I nuzzled into her neck and breathed deeply. She smelled like a flower show that was hit by a pheromone bomb. And I was the lonely bee looking for a petal to land on.

"But over the summer—" I groaned.

"Nothing happened over the summer. Do you hear me? Nothing."

"So you're going to make me wait until marriage? You really think that's a viable option in this day and age?"

"No, I didn't say that. I just said that I'm not ready yet, after all that's gone on between us."

"Don't you want to?"

"More than you can possibly imagine."

"When are you going back to San Diego?"

"I don't know. Pretty soon, I guess. I have to wrap things up there so I can move back here."

"Even after what happened, with the whole near-death experience again, being held at gunpoint by a maniac and drug dealer, escaping from a burning house?"

"There's something very familiar and comforting about that," she sighed. "It reminds me of my family."

"You are one morbid chick."

"Yeah, and you're stuck with me."

"Didn't you like San Diego?"

"Yes and no. It's great in some ways but it's kind of lame. Definitely no exploding houses. Just lots of tan, muscular, insanely hot guys."

"Hand me my phone."

"Why?"

"I want to see if your dad's offer is still available."

"Jerk."

"Fatso."

Aria took my hand and put it on her smooth, flat belly. "You really think I'm fat? Guess I'll never wear that bikini around you, I wouldn't want to make you puke."

"I'll try accepting you as you are. Speaking of bikinis, I think I'd like to take a vacation. I've never been on a real vacation, you know."

"Never?"

"Nope."

"You poor boy. Where would you like to go?"

"I was thinking maybe the Caribbean."

"I see. You wouldn't happen to be thinking of St. John, would you?"

"As a matter of fact, I was."

"That's great!" She jumped off the cot and started pacing. "I know a place there, Caneel Bay, it's absolutely amazing. We can rent a car and start looking for your dad. I can book it today, right now if you want."

"No."

"Why not? Don't you want to find him?

"Yes. But you're not paying for me. I need to save the money first, which will take time, considering the guitar and the rest of Scarlet's memorabilia went up in flames."

"Serves her right, trying to seduce my man like that."

"Could you stop thinking only about yourself? I could have really used that money, you know. Hopefully, the garage sale will still come together and I can make enough to take a trip. Assuming my probation officer will let me, which is doubtful, considering any day now he's going to arrest me for blowing a pee test."

"See? That dirty hippie girl was bad for you, just like I told you."

There was a knock on the door.

"You expecting company? Another yoga teacher with a bad back perhaps?"

I got up and opened the door. Daddy-O was standing there. He wasn't smiling.

"Speak of the devil," I said.

"Am I interrupting something?"

"No, just my plan for escaping with my moll here. Aria, you remember Officer D'Addario, my probation officer?"

He went over and shook her hand.

"Nice to see you again."

"Likewise."

Daddy-O turned and gave me a look. "You've been busy lately, haven't you?"

"Sort of."

"I heard all about it. Drug lab, explosion, two more stiffs, which makes four total, and a sleazy biker gang. And everyone is saying that you acted like a hero again. When are you ever going to learn?"

"I think Martin was the real hero. I was just there to get a guitar appraised."

Daddy-O shook his head. "I can see why you don't return my calls. Anyway, I was on my way to my folks' place and since you are too busy to call me back, I thought I'd stop by." He motioned his head in Aria's direction. "Do you want me to tell you privately?"

"She can stay," I said, a lump in my throat.

"If you say so."

"Look," I blurted out, "I'm sorry, I don't know how it got in there, but I asked Scarlet about the aspirin because I hurt my arm again when the fat guy tried running me down and she was on the phone so when she said sink and pointed to the kitchen I just assumed she meant kitchen sink but she really meant bathroom sink—dumb, right? But totally true oh God please don't lock me up I'll do anything to prove it to you I'm trying so hard even though I took Prince Shieldheart and tried breaking into the store and stole Pete's iPhone I thought it might be useful for evidence but then I had the guitar and Scarlet got a text from China and oh please don't lock me up at least until I've made it with my girlfriend in a tent please."

"Yeah, that tent thing ain't happening," Aria said.

Daddy-O stared at me, blinked, then turned to Aria.

"You really ought to do something to help him relax."

"I don't know, I kind of like him like this."

"Are you finished?"

"I don't know," I gasped. "You tell me."

"It came back clean. Everything is fine."

"It what?"

"The test. You're clean. Relax."

"Why the hell didn't you say that on your message?"

"I'm not allowed to leave the results on voicemail, because the results are confidential and voice mail isn't secure. It's a legal thing. I have to tell clients in person, or at least speak to them on the phone. Which you would have known if you bothered calling me back." He gave me a sidelong glance. "Were you expecting a different result?"

"No."

He nodded slowly. "Sure. Okay. Have fun, you two."

Daddy-O waved good-bye and left. I closed the door and leaned against it.

"I can't believe they didn't find anything."

"It's a gift," Aria sighed. "Don't examine it too closely. Just be thankful."

"I'm thankful. Now move over."

I'd just gotten back to spooning Aria when there was another knock on the door. I expected Daddy-O, but Aku was there instead.

"Do you have a moment?"

"Sure, come on in."

Aku saw Aria and his face lit up, then he bowed.

"It's so nice to see you again."

"It's good to see you too. How's the Wizard business?"

"Fine, thank you for asking. But I must say that Bert was in a terrible state the whole time you were away. I think you're very good for him." He looked at me. "Was I mistaken or did I see Officer D'Addario leaving?"

"He was just here with the results of my urine test. I still can't believe it."

"I thought it might be about that. That's why I stopped by. I have a confession to make. The other day, when you came into the bathroom while I was in the shower—"

"You didn't tell me about that either," Aria muttered to me. "Did you take him to Brooklyn too?"

"As I was saying, when you came in to use the toilet, I felt I was rather rude in the way that I expressed my displeasure. Then I noticed the sample cup on the sink counter, and I figured it was probably related to your probation requirements. I recalled that when I saw you with Scarlet the evening before, at the 4-D party, you seemed to be under the influence of something stronger than my Night Vision potion."

"You never took me to a party," Aria muttered again.

"Quiet," I ordered her.

"Anyway, it occurred to me that you might have been under the influence of some kind of illicit substance, which explained why you were so distracted when you came into the bathroom. I'd never seen you behave like that before. When I got out of the shower I saw that you'd filled the sample cup but left it there. I decided to be on the safe side and I dumped yours out and refilled it with, um—my own supply, if you will."

"You swapped pee so I wouldn't get busted?"

"I felt it was advisable, under the circumstances. I have nothing in my system stronger than herbal tea, so there was no danger there."

"You're awesome, thanks. And speaking of awesome, that little finger flasher you gave me probably saved my life, and maybe several other people as well."

Aku bowed. "Always glad to be of service." He looked at the TV on the dresser. The blonde psychic was rubbing her temples. "I'm not sure I approve of your taste in television shows, however. Such people give our calling a bad name. But you are very lucky to have a woman who gives you such generous gifts."

"I'm glad someone appreciates me," Aria said. I turned her on her back and kissed her hard. She pushed me off and sat up. "What the heck?"

I looked over my shoulder. Aku was gone.

"I'd like to see the Long Island Medium do that," I said.

We went back to kissing. It was just getting hot and heavy when there was another knock.

"You should just leave the stupid door open," Aria groaned. "Save people the trouble."

"I'll get rid of whoever it is," I said. I walked over to the door. "Who is it?"

A muffled voice answered from behind the door. "Master Shambles?"

"Who?"

"I'm looking for Master Shambles."

"I think he means you," Aria said.

I opened the door a crack. A dwarf was standing there. He had a big beard and was wearing a helmet and armor.

"I come on a quest of the utmost urgency," the dwarf said.

"Look, man, I'm sorry about what happened to Prince Shieldhart, but you guys have to get over it already."

"I know not of what you speak. My mission is unrelated to what you describe."

"Then what do you want?"

The dwarf handed me a small suede bag, tied at the top with a leather string. I opened it and pulled out a gold coin. I peeled off the gold foil and ate the chocolate inside.

"My favorite."

"Who is it?" asked Aria. "What's going on?"

"Hold on," I told the dwarf. I closed the door and turned to her.

"It's a dwarf with an axe and a bag of chocolate. He says he needs my help."

"Then I guess you'd better let him in, hometown hero."

I opened the door a crack and stuck my head back out.

"Not interested, sorry. You can take your chocolate back."

"Give me those," Aria said, jumping out of the cot. She took a handful of the coins and started peeling. "I love these."

"But he wants to hire me!"

"Then let the guy in, let's hear what he has to say. What's the worst that can happen?"

I was about to say something when she wrapped her arm around my waist. A million microscopic hamsters started doing the happy dance on my spine again. Whatever the guy wanted, it couldn't hurt to listen. I opened the door and the dwarf came in.

THE END

ABOUT THE AUTHOR

 Tim Hall was a journalist, musician, bike messenger and moving man before turning to the lucrative world of independent publishing. *Tie Died* is the second in his Bert Shambles mysteries. The first was *Dead Stock*. Hall lives and works in New York City. He can be found online at timhallbooks.wordpress.com. (Photo credit: Yasmeen Anderson Photography)

Made in the USA
Middletown, DE
07 May 2015